8/14

MONS
HUNT
UNLIMITED

D1409329

THE UNDEAD AND
WATER BEASTS
BY JOHN GATEHOUSE AND DAVE WINDETT

Per
tiv
i. tr
di e.
lum
f.

PSS!
PRICE STERN SLOAN
An Imprint of Penguin Group (USA) LLC

For Abbie, Jordon, Grace, and Melissa—JG

To my parents and my brother—DMW

PRICE STERN SLOAN
Published by the Penguin Group
Penguin Group (USA) LLC, 375 Hudson Street, New York, New York 10014, USA

USA | Canada | UK | Ireland | Australia | New Zealand | India | South Africa | China

penguin.com
A Penguin Random House Company

Library of Congress Cataloging-in-Publication Data is available.

ISBN 978-0-8431-6980-5   10 9 8 7 6 5 4 3 2 1

INTRODUCTION

*He who fights with monsters
should be careful lest he thereby
become a monster.*

—Friedrich Wilhelm Nietzsche (1844-1900)

—German philosopher

Fair warning: this book is **GRUESOME!!** There are lashings of spilled blood and eviscerated (ripped-out) entrails on show. So if you're of a more sensitive (wimpy) nature, we suggest you go read something else instead! (This book is about **MONSTERS!!!**)

For the more adventurous souls among us, you are holding in your hands a book that could literally *change your life*. It could also get you brutally and horrifically killed . . . but no one lives forever, right? (Aside from the terrifying undead. And those creepoids have to *die* before they un-live, so they don't count!)

Want to travel the world? Have thrills and chills? Fight all sorts of creatures? Then join the International Federation of Monster Hunters. Yep, we monster hunters have our own special club—and all this could be yours! (But be warned: Monster hunting is dirty, dangerous, foul, and fetid work. But it's one heck of a lot more fun than flipping burgers for a living.)

First up, ignore those who scoff at news stories of giant sea serpents, bloodsucking vampires, malignant ghosts, and flesh-eating zombies. These horrible creatures *do* exist. They have since before the dawn of time. The soulless undead! Vicious Elementals! Hideous man-monsters! Deadly demons! Nightmarish animals! Terrifying water beasts! Heart-stopping phantasms! They are all here on Earth, hunting down their favorite prey—humans!

Reckon you have the courage to drive a stake through a vampire's heart? Or to lop off the head of a zombie with a battle-ax? Then you're exactly the kind of crazy dude or dudette we're looking for! Walk with us on the wild side and we'll introduce you to the bloodcurdling supernatural world that exists outside your own front door!

From the famous to the obscure, from the bizarre to the ridiculous, the most dangerous (and not-so-dangerous) frights of the supernatural world are listed, examined, and unmasked inside the pages of Monster Hunters Unlimited!

We reveal the true facts about each monster that coldly stalks the long, dark nights. You will learn their origins, locations, appearance, strengths, weaknesses, powers, and fear factor!

You'll also be presented with the kick-butt weapons and techniques you'll need to track down, capture, and—if necessary—*destroy* these beasts! A wooden stake, magic potions and incantations, silver bullets, a sword and battle-ax, and holy water and religious symbols are but a few of the items necessary for a successful hunt!

This whacked-out, amped-up series isn't merely about the monsters. Get ready to meet thirteen-year-old Tobias Toombes, who runs his own hard-core monster blog! Intrepid reporter of the best-selling *Weekly World Examiner* Neela Nightshade! And special agent Rock Hardy of a clandestine US government agency the C.B.I. (Central Bureau of Investigations)!

These are but three of the many true-grit monster hunters whose exploits we'll be celebrating in these pages!

Our case studies investigate true stories of encounters with a menagerie of unbelievable monsters. These files include ships' logs, police and medical reports, ancient legends, sagas and folktales, government brochures, séance transcriptions, magazine articles, book excerpts, radio and TV broadcasts, scientific surveys, court cases, interviews, historical journals, diaries and letters, and much more!

Wait until you meet the famous historical figures who have either seen or believed in the existence of monsters. Leonardo da Vinci! Homer! Captain James Cook! Saint Columba and Saint Martha! Alfred, Lord Tennyson! Charles Darwin! Joseph Stalin! King Arthur!

This series is interactive, which means that you have to share your monster-hunting stories with us: your successes and failures, the good and the bad. (We've all had them!)

Follow Tobias's lead and start your own monster blog, listing all the information about the various monsters you hunt—including your reports, photos, and artwork of the monsters you've tracked down, and your own brilliant methods for capturing and/or killing them!

Start a scrapbook of newspaper cuttings, write a daily diary of your activities (this way, if you get squished by a monster, your own final words can be used your eulogy—hey, we're just saying!), film a monster hunt and upload it to the Internet. Whatever you can think of to promote yourself as a monster hunter—do it! (But make sure it's legal!)

We have given each monster in this book a fear-factor rating. If you disagree with our evaluations, write in and tell us why. We love a good debate!

And collate your own Monster Fear Factor Top Ten list. Which monsters do *you* reckon are the scariest and most deadly? We want to know.

As we continually warn newbie monsters hunters, don't believe all you read—except for what's in this book, obviously—so quadruple-check your facts! You don't want to call a live press conference only to discover that your "facts" are fiction. Right there, that's your career *zombified*—i.e., stone dead!

Monster hunting is the real deal! So take care, have fun, and enjoy the ride! And watch out for any demonic shape-shifter disguised as your grandma! (They're sneaky that way!)

DISCLAIMER: Anyone who goes monster hunting does so at their own risk. We cannot be held responsible for our readers turning into vampires, werewolves, zombies, or other assorted nasties.

TABLE OF CONTENTS

THE UNDEAD

There are more dead people than living. And their numbers are increasing. The living are getting rarer.

—Eugène Ionesco (1909–1994)—Romanian-born
playwright and dramatist

In the murky, twilight world of the monster hunter, the nomenclature (tag, term, name, call it what you will) *undead* refers to any human (and to a lesser extent, animal) that has died and returns to a chilling un-life through supernatural forces such as sorcery, witchcraft, or vampirism.

The official name for these reanimated corpses is *revenant*. This covers all undead creatures, whether they are *incorporeal*, a soul or spirit without an actual solid body (ghosts and poltergeists for example), or *corporeal*, meaning they have a physical body (your basic vampires and zombies). The term originates from the Latin word *revenire*, meaning to come back. (The things you learn . . . !)

For this book, we have focused on corporeal undead. For all the latest intel on ghosts, spirits, poltergeists, ectoplasms, and other sundry ghoulish incorporeal apparitions, check out other titles in this killer series!

The undead are a global phenomenon that have existed since humans first started swinging through trees screeching "Eeek! Eeek!" alongside their fellow hairy hominid (great ape) pals.

They were especially active in medieval Britain, in a period known as the High Middle Ages (the eleventh through twelfth centuries). Twelfth-century English historian and Augustinian canon (top church guy) William Parvus—aka William of Newburgh, or plain Willy to his friends (c. 1136–1198)—wrote in the 1190s that "one would not easily believe that corpses come out of their graves and wander around, animated by some evil spirit, to terrorize or harm the living, unless there were many cases in our times, supported by ample testimony."

There are two main types of corporeal undead: the aforementioned and legendary vamps and zombies, and the scarier but much less famous *psychopomps*. (In Greek, *psuchopompós*, meaning "guide of souls." Why Greek? Because the ancient Geeks were freaky-deaky keen on the afterlife!)

Psychopomps are mega-cruel creeps who only ever appear seconds before some poor peep is literally about to *zonk the big one, kick the bucket, head for the boneyard, buy the farm, cash in one's chips, breathe one's last,* start *pushing up daisies,* become *worm food,* and generally *die!* They come to gather the departing soul and escort it (a-kickin' an' a-screamin', we'd imagine) toward wherever it's supposed to go: up, down, or anywhere in between!

In the following pages you are going to meet the world's nastiest, meanest, most totally vicious and utterly evil undead around!

There's German vampire/zombie (yep, a two-in-one) Nachzehrer who feasts on both the living and on rotting corpses! (*Ewww!*) The all-dat Filipino killer baby Tiyanak! The giant—and we mean *GIANT*!!—skeletal Japanese nightmare Gashadokuro!

Bloody Mary from the United Kingdom will tear you to pieces the moment she sets eyes on you! Monstrous cool and über-psychotic vampire Nelapsi can happily butcher an entire village in a single night! The Caribbean serves up the vampire fireball Soucouyant! From France comes the most savage zombie of all—Craquehhe! And the undead Norse Viking warrior Draugr kills you in your sleep!

Want to try your hand at hunting the undead? Willing to risk becoming undead yourself? (That is if you even *survive* the encounter!) We admire your guts! (And so will any undead that gets its decomposing hands on you!) Good luck!

ADZE

Let's start our monster hunting at the Cradle of Humanity—*Africa*!

The world's second-largest continent is home to many of the goriest and most predatory supernatural creatures around.

Who's the worst? We reckon that fiend numero uno on the list has to be the vampiric *Adze*!

This blood-guzzling nightmare preys exclusively on the people of the Ewe tribe, who are located on the plains of the Volta region of Ghana, Southern Togo, Benin, and Nigeria.

And what is an Adze's favorite dish of the day? *Children!*

A shape-changer, the Adze takes many insect forms, its preference being that of a tiny firefly with an elephant-like trunk.

Unlike true fireflies, whose bodies contain highly toxic chemicals called *lucibufagins* (LBFs) that kill some animals that try to eat them, the Adze prefers a more gruesome method of dispatching its victims.

When night's velvet curtain falls, the Adze flits soundlessly through closed doors, landing on a sleeping child's lips. Biting through the soft pulpy flesh, it sucks the body dry of blood. Death is inevitable!

Other times, the Adze will take possession of a victim's mind, causing them to bring terrible illness and bad luck to family, friends, and neighbors.

Occasionally, sorcerers allow themselves to become a human host to an Adze. They are rewarded with supernatural powers and abilities such as shape-changing and mind control.

However, if they are captured, they immediately revert back to human form, and the magic is lost to them. They will then face the terrible wrath of their somewhat irate tribesmen!

Before deciding that a can of bug spray and a flyswatter is all you'll need to kill an Adze, think again!

When trapped, the Adze will swiftly change from firefly back to quasi-human form, a hideous hunchback with long razor-sharp talons and superhuman strength.

Leaping upon you, it will slice open your chest, hungrily feasting on your heart and liver, perhaps partaking of a glass or two of your warm gushing blood to wash down its meal. (Not a vegetarian, then!)

What gives the Adze its strength and power is the juicy fresh blood of young children.

If it can't find a kid to snack on, it will consume vast quantities of coconut water and palm oil. In doing so, the Adze will become progressively weaker, allowing it to be easily overcome and destroyed.

WARNING! If humans try to interfere with its blood-supping, the Adze will release virulent diseases from the pores of its body that can decimate an entire village!

Case Study 633/17a

This may come as a shock to some of you monster hunters out there, but for millennia the Internet was *not* the preferred choice for social networking.

On the African continent, after a hard day's work, villagers would sit around the campfire listening to folktales told by the tribal elders. Each of these stories contained a moral, and they rarely had a happy ending.

During our investigations, we paid a visit to the Ewe people and were kindly granted permission to record one such folktale, which we reproduce below.

The Firefly Who Came to Dinner

One warm summer night, a firefly came to the village to feast.

This was no ordinary firefly. He was an Adze, one of the terrifying undead!

The Adze flew through the door of a hut. Asleep on a bed was a boy of eleven. His leg was broken.

"Not as young as I would like, but he will have to do," said the Adze, landing on the boy's face. "I hunger fiercely!"

The boy woke up with a start!

"Do not drink my blood, Adze," the boy pleaded. "My family returns tomorrow from a trip. My younger brother will be with them. He is only three."

"Three?" cried the Adze excitedly. "His blood will taste so much sweeter than yours. But I cannot wait until tomorrow. I must feast tonight!"

The boy hobbled over to a large jar and pulled off the lid. "Drink this coconut water tonight, and come back tomorrow for my brother."

The Adze could not resist the coconut water and drank every last drop.

The next night, the Adze came to the hut again. "Where is your brother?" demanded the Adze. "I want to sup upon his sweet blood."

"My family has been delayed," said the boy, opening a large jar. "They will be back in the morning. For now, enjoy this delicious palm oil."

The Adze could not resist the palm oil and devoured it quickly.

Each night for a whole week the Adze returned, and the boy told him that his family had been delayed.

Instead of drinking the blood of a young child, which would make him stronger, the Adze consumed vast amounts of coconut water and palm oil, which made him progressively weaker.

Before his next visit, the boy collected all the coconut water and palm oil in the village. The greedy Adze drank it all.

"Oh, I am so weak I cannot fly," groaned the Adze, falling to the ground. "When will your family return home?"

The door swung open and the boy's little brother appeared.

"They came back this morning," replied the boy.

He watched, smiling coldly, as his brother raised his foot, then brought it crashing down on the Adze, killing him instantly.

ADZE FACT FILE

Location: Ghana, Southern Togo, Benin, Nigeria
Appearance: Any insect, but prefers the body of a firefly with an elephant's trunk; hunchback with razor-sharp talons
Strength: Superhuman strength when human; bug-size, not so much!
Weaknesses: Coconut water, palm oil
Powers: Shape-changing, flight, intangibility (ability to pass through solid objects), the spreading of virulent disease, annoying buzzing sound
Fear Factor: 73

HOW TO CAPTURE AN ADZE

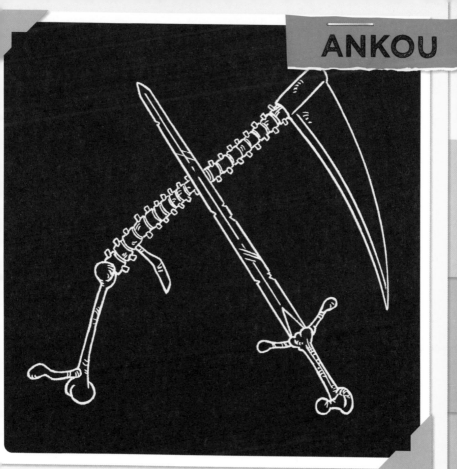

Check out one of the most hard-core and fatal supernatural creeps a monster hunter can face—*Ankou, Harvester of Souls!*

There are numerous soul gatherers—psychopomps—out there in Spooksville, of which the Ankou (a.k.a. Aräwn) is considered by many to be Top Dog.

If you're unlucky enough to cross paths, it means you are literally moments away from your own death! (So best update that last will & testament before tracking him down! Your chances of surviving an encounter with Ankou ain't good!)

As responsible monster hunters, we could never suggest that you purposely go mano a mano with this undead terror.

Nonetheless, in our business and with the type of bloodcurdling demonic nasties we regularly go up against, there's a better than average chance that the Ankou will be lurking somewhere in the shadows, awaiting your approaching demise.

The Ankou changes its soul on a yearly basis, as it is the last person in a city or county to die each year. Upon demise, Ankou is assigned to collect all the souls released the following year and escort them to death's door. Only then may the Ankou itself find eternal rest.

Man, woman, skeleton, or shadow, often sporting long white or silvery hair, the Ankou's usual attire is an ebony cloak or jacket and a large-brimmed hat pulled down to conceal its features. If that's not enough recognition factor, it carries a scythe or sword with a handle made from human bone!

Controversially, some Christian scholars claim that the Ankou is related to Cain—yep, that "smashed his brother's head in with a rock" Old Testament biblical dude. Others say that it is Cain himself, cursed to walk the Earth forevermore collecting souls as penance.

Utterly devoid of mercy, Ankou will cut the life thread of anyone—children and babies included! It was once heard to mirthlessly chuckle: "There's always room for one more body in my cart."

Case Study 811/29a

Tobias Toombes is a thirteen-year-old monster hunter who posts a weekly blog.

Toby is one of few mortals to have had a run-in with the Ankou and survive!

I'd been keeping watch on the home of Old Mrs. Stinkybottom—well, that's what I call her! Jeez, her atomic farts could flatten a small country! *Phooaah!*—because rumor had it she was about to kick the bucket, and I wanted to be around when she did.

Dead people attract the supernatural boogers, and I was after the biggest demon booger of them all—*Ankou!*

Anyways, it was 2:17 a.m. on a cold winter's morning, and I was freezing my butt off hiding out in her back garden. All through the evening there had been a parade of family and friends calling on her digs, wailing and sobbing and

generally boo-hoo-hoo-ing because they knew Mrs. Stinkybottom was on her way out.

All had been hushed for a while, then suddenly—no joking!—a cold wind began to whistle up and this frigid white mist descended from nowhere, but *only* around Stinkybottom's pad. Man, it was *glacial! Brrr!*

Then I heard it! The hair-raising *clip-clop, clip-clop* of horses' hooves on pavement and the fear-inducing *Creeaak! Creeaak! Creeaak!* from the wheels of Ankou's wooden death cart!

From out of the mist appeared two spectral pale horses, one old and thin, the other young and strong, snorting plumes of fire and brimstone from their nostrils.

They were pulling an ancient coal-black wagon that was already laden down with the wailing soul-carcasses of the recently departed, all piled on top of one another like a sack o' turnips!

On each side of the cart walked a tall, translucent figure, their faces hidden by hoodies.

And riding on top of the cart, gently whipping the horses along, was The Man himself! *Ankou—King of the Dead!*

He was a tall, cadaverous figure with sickly pale skin, long silvery hair, and empty eye sockets that burned with a fiery light. He wore a long black trench coat, his face partial hidden by a wide-brimmed hat. Resting over one shoulder was a gleaming scythe.

But the kicker was his head!

17

Reining in the cart outside SB's crib, Ankou turned his head a *complete 360* degrees before gazing directly—at me!

Seriously, I almost filled my pants!

"*Tobias Toombes*," the Ankou intoned in a deathly chill voice. "*You are interfering in matters which do not concern you. Your fate is foretold to me, but this is not your time. Not yet. But soon, perhaps . . . yes, very soon . . .*"

And with that, I felt a sharp punch in my chest! I jerked back and opened my eyes . . . to find myself in my bed, tangled up in my blanket, my rotten black cat Hellspawn standing on top of me, hissing loudly.

It wasn't a dream! I swear.

An old Irish proverb says, "When Ankou comes, he will not go away empty." Mrs. Stinkybottom died that same night. They say she went off with a look of unholy terror on her face, as if she had seen something— or *someone*!—who had scared the life outta her!

THE ANKOU FACT FILE

Location: Celtic countries, notably Ireland and Wales and Cornwall in the United Kingdom, Brittany in France, and also parts of the US.

Appearance: Scary!

Strength: The Ankou may look scrawny, but it is Death's disciple, so we reckon it's got the juice to take on all comers.

Weaknesses: None! (But if you ever discover one, let us know!)

Powers: Lethal death-touch

Fear Factor: 999

HOW TO DEFEAT THE ANKOU

You can't! So in the immortal words of cowards everywhere—run, run, run away!! (Hey, we're in the monster-hunting biz, not the "let's die early" biz!)

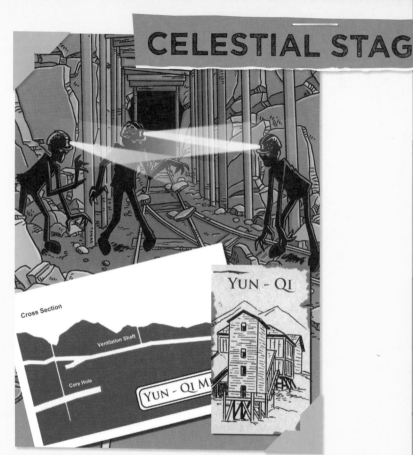

Cool moniker, eh? Shame these creepoids aren't heaven-sent, nor do they resemble that proud beast of the forest!

It is the group name given to reanimated corpses of Chinese miners.

(FYI: China is the world's largest coal producer and consumer, swallowing up over 47 percent of the world's total coal output. Approximately 5 million people work in the Chinese coal industry. Each year, more than a thousand workers are tragically killed in mine accidents. Our advice? Don't be a miner in China.)

Across the Yunnan province, when the tunnels they are working in collapse, miners are quite literally *buried alive*. Unable to escape, they may face a slow, agonizing, mind-shattering death.

Days later, their corpses are sparked back to un-life by the five special metals found exclusively in these mines. They become *kiang si*—corpse-demons!

Descriptions of Celestial Stag vary wildly, for no one has yet seen one clearly and lived to tell the tale.

It is said that they are "hidden murky demons" (well, gee, thanks, that's a great help!) or else amorphous shadow-beings. All we can say for sure is you'll know one when you run into it! (Of course, by then it may be too late!)

Unlike many of their undead brethren, Celestial Stag retain their intelligence and power of speech. If they meet living miners, they plead desperately to be taken back up to the surface, promising the workers unimaginable wealth in gold.

Realizing that allowing these nightmarish zombies to escape and stalk the land might not go down too well with the locals, most miners refuse to help. Bad move! Celestial Stags do not take rejection kindly.

They turn violent, jeering and tormenting the miners before chasing them through the tunnels. Once trapped, the frightened men face death through unspeakable tortures. (So let's not speak about them!)

Other times, miners have tricked Celestial Stag into showing them where their gold is kept, and then snuck off with it. (Neat!)

If you come across a lone Stag and you're with a gang of miners, overpower him, tether him to the mine floor, and build a clay wall around him. Or place a lighted lamp above the Stag. This will allow his restless spirit to finally move on. (Ahh! Don't you love a happy ending?!)

WARNING! A Stag that makes it to the surface is bad news for everyone! The moment they stagger free of the miners and are touched by fresh air, their clothes, flesh, and bones melt into a huge poisonous mass of gloopy black goo that releases a "rancid, putrid stench" and rot, spreading hideous contagious diseases and instant death across the land!

Case Study 969/77cs

We've managed to obtain a top secret government report concerning an accident that took place in a Chinese mine. It makes for interesting reading! The Chinese government, naturally, denies all knowledge of Celestial Stag. (Well, they would, wouldn't they?!)

Mining, Accident, & Injury Report
People's Republic of China

August 9

On August 8, at approximately 7:09 a.m., one miner was killed and another three injured after a small explosion in Tunnel 16 of the Yun-Qi mine. They were working underground, mining for gold deposits. A faulty explosive or buildup of inflammable gas may be to blame.

This comes on the anniversary of a much more catastrophic explosion that saw the deaths of seventeen miners. They were tragically entombed when the tunnel in which they were working collapsed, sealing them behind a wall of solid rock. Rescuers tried to tunnel through the rock, but to no avail.

The miners involved in yesterday's accident claim that they were making their way out of the tunnel, carrying the dead and wounded, when they found their way blocked by a group of what they call "shadow-creatures."

These creatures were humanoid in shape, yet had no distinguishing features that the miners could make out. These "creatures" supposedly begged the miners to take them back to the surface world. If they did so, the creatures would reward them with gold. If not, the creatures would kill them all.

The miners led these "creatures" to an elevator, pleading that they be allowed go up first to give aid to their injured colleagues. The creatures agreed, and the miners returned to the surface, 1.8 miles above.

As promised, they sent the elevator back down for the creatures. But as it made its way back to the surface, one of the men threw down explosives. The detonation ripped apart the elevator. The wreckage fell back down the mine shaft before a second explosion caused a massive cave-in, sealing the mine forever.

This investigator concludes that the miners were suffering from hallucinations from the build up of gases. No one admits responsibility for the elevator explosion, and I can see no hope of bringing charges against the man or men involved. I recommend instant dismissal of them all.

CELESTIAL STAG FACT FILE

Location: Yunnan province, China
Appearance: Shadowy demons
Strength: Strong adult human
Weaknesses: Fresh air, clay
Power: Spreading fatal disease and rot
Fear Factor: 47

WHAT TO DO WITH GLOOPY GOO (SORRY, CELESTIAL STAG)

Once you've tricked a Celestial Stag above ground and he turns into a mass of gloopy goo, what do you do with it?

Our advice? Sell it to the local goth kids to paint their bedroom walls black! (It has the added bonus of being tainted with the soul of the dead! *Woo-ooo-oooh!*)

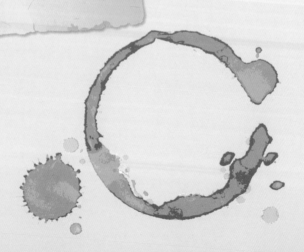

A Draugr (pronounced *Droo-Gore*, plural *Draugar*) is the ancient Norse word for "ghost." It is the reanimated body of a dead Viking. The creature is sometimes named *Aptrgangr*, which means "again-walker" or even more wicked, "one who walks after death"!

History note: The word *Viking* comes from the Old Norse language and means "a pirate raid." Warriors who went off in ships to raid other countries were said to be "going on a Viking"! The Vikings were the BMOC (Big Men on Campus) from about AD 700–1100.

There are two types, a land-Draugr and a sea-Draugr. The Draugar are first mentioned in the Sagas of Icelanders, a series of thrilling stories that were written during the thirteenth and early fourteenth centuries based on events that happened in Iceland around the year 1000.

It wasn't long before the Draugar were sighted in other Nordic countries, such as Norway,

Sweden, and Denmark, and as far away as Britain and France.

Many Vikings who fell on the bloodstained battlefields were honored with burial in tomb-like barrows (large earth mounds).

Their restless spirits, however, grew jealous of the living having fun while they were rotting in the ground. They escaped their earthly imprisonment by turning into wisps of smoke before reforming to take murderous revenge.

A Draugr has many unworldly powers and abilities, including turning into a giant, controlling the weather, entering your dreams to kill you, and shape-shifting.

They are especially slick at transforming into a large seal, a gray horse with a broken back and no ears or tail, or a cat that will sit on your chest, growing increasingly heavier until it crushes the life out of you!

If hunting a Draugr is top of your to-do list (Respect!), first investigate a recent sighting, and then camp out beside its burial mound. A Draugr will wait until the dead of night before paying an unwelcome call on its neighbors.

Chances are, unless you're an experienced monster hunter you're going to meet a grisly fate.

You might be crushed between its gargantuan hands, have your flesh devoured and your blood drunk dry, or you may even be devoured whole! Any humans or animals in proximity to a Draugr will turn instantly mad and die.

To defeat a Draugr, you must first be pure of heart. Face off against it while it's in its giant form and wrestle it to the ground–with your *bare hands*! (*Pft!* Easy!)

Then the monster must be decapitated with its own weapons (sword or battle-ax, take your pick) and its body quickly cremated, its ashes disposed at sea.

Case Study 103/22d

This report by top journalist Neela Nightshade
recently appeared in the best-selling tabloid
newspaper the Weekly World Examiner.

Attack of the Monster Viking

Exclusive Report by Neela Nightshade
Supernatural Correspondent
KAANTSPELLIT, Norway, April II

This small Norwegian fishing village in the back end of nowhere has a bad smell to it, and I don't mean of mackerel. It is the overpowering stench— of death!

In the past few weeks, seven people have been slaughtered during the night. Their bodies were torn asunder and partially consumed.

The locals know who the culprit is—a Draugr! A nightmarish undead creature!

"Most definitely it is the dreaded sea-Draugr, no?" claims one frightened old man. "They are the poor unfortunates who have drowned at sea. Their tormented spirits rise again, transformed into seaweed forms, or else with a serpent's body and a massive seaweed head!"

Others describe the sea-Draugr as a headless fisherman dressed in oilskins. Who knows for sure?

My investigations stalled when the villagers refused to be interviewed. They fear the wrath of the Draugr!

Then I got a lucky break. A woman whose husband was one of the victims was willing to meet on the outskirts of town and speak on the record.

As I was arriving at my rendezvous, dark clouds formed as if from nowhere, turning day into night. A freezing, howling wind whipped up, and savage lightning shredded the sky.

Struggling forward through the maelstrom, I perceived a young woman at the end of the street. My contact!

Before I could signal my presence, a huge form materialized from nowhere, growing to gigantic proportions, a battered Viking's helmet perched upon its head: a land-Draugr!

Its desiccated, diseased skin was of a deathly blue hue. Soulless eyes glared threateningly at the terrified woman, who shrank back, helpless.

Roaring angrily, the Draugr raised its mighty arm to smite her. Snapping off a shot with my pocket camera, I screamed for the woman to run—too late!

As the Draugr disappeared once more, the woman collapsed in a heap, her hair turned white and her mind forever shattered with pure, unadulterated fear!

Another victim of . . . the Draugr!

DRAUGR FACT FILE

Location: Iceland, Finland, Denmark, Norway, Sweden, Britain, France
Appearance: A giant Undead Viking!
Strength: Superhuman
Weaknesses: Cold iron, a hero utterly pure of heart, decapitation with its own weapon
Powers: The ability to grow to giant size, intangibility, weather control, shape-shifting, precognition (seeing into the future), turning to wisps of smoke, entering victims' dreams, creating total darkness, spreading deadly disease, sorcery
Fear Factor: 97.3

HOW TO KILL A DRAUGR

1. Throw a wild party close to his tomb-barrow.
2. When he comes over to complain about the noise, tell him to stop being such an complainer and join in the fun.
3. While he's boogying down on the dance floor, take his mighty battle-ax, creep up behind him, and—SHUNK!—chop off his head!
4. String up the head from the ceiling and play a really ghoulish game of piñata! (First one to bash out his eyeballs wins!)

For a new hunter eager to nab his or her first monster, the best country to head to is Japan (aka *Nippon* or *Nihon* in Japanese).

Located in the Pacific Ocean, Japan is an archipelago consisting of 6,852 separate islands. Almost 70 percent of the country is mountainous, and there are around two hundred volcanoes, of which Mount Fuji, at 12,389 feet, is the highest.

Many of the 127,817,300-plus inhabitants will nervously whisper to you about their terrifying encounters with the numerous bloodthirsty supernatural creatures that prowl the lands.

Forget Godzilla; the Land of the Rising Sun has a huge abundance of spirits, obake, cacodemons, elementals, shape-shifters, Kaiju, winged creatures, suijins, man-beasts, archfiends, and the horrifying undead that take great delight in preying on—and devouring—helpless humans!

The deadliest *yōkai*—the Japanese word for demon, monster, or ghoul—is the frightfully fearsome *Gashadokuro*!

You've heard the expression that "everyone has a skeleton in his closet"? Well, if you have a skeleton the size of Gashadokuro, you really have been up to no good! Because these guys are freaking *ginormous* to the power of 10!

Gashadokuro (aka *Odokuro*) are skeletons of monstrous proportions. Some may reach the dizzying heights of ninety feet or more!

Biology note: Human babies are born with approximately 300 bones. Over time, many of these fuse together, creating a skeleton of 206 bones. These range from the almost microscopic ossicles of the inner ear to the femur (the thigh bone) which is the longest, heaviest, and strongest bone in the body. The femur bone makes up 26 percent of a person's height. So just imagine the size of a Gashadokuro femur bone! Yowsers!

Gashadokuro are the remains of people who died hideously painful deaths through famine or on blood-soaked battlefields, or bodies that were not given proper respect or a decent burial.

Their restless spirits, understandably peeved at being dead (and who wouldn't be?), collect their bones and fuse them together into the giant form of Gashadokuro. The monster then wanders the cities and villages at midnight, searching for the living upon which to take its dread revenge!

Despite its immense size, its supernatural ability to walk with silent steps allows Gashadokuro to sneak up on you.

Your only warning will be a sharp ringing sensation in your ears. By then it's too late! The Gashadokuro will grab you in its bony hand, crushing out your breath. Lifting you up to its cavernous mouth, its razor-sharp teeth will tear off your head. Gashadokuro will then slake its immense thirst by drinking your body dry of blood.

Some Gashadokuro go further and eat the victim whole, crunching up their bones, which it then absorbs into itself, growing ever larger.

The irony of death by Gashadokuro is that once your headless body has decomposed and mere skeletal remains exist, your own restless spirit will want bloody revenge.

It will seek out other victims and together your bones will merge to create yet another Gashadokuro. And so the endless cycle continues . . .

There is but one way to destroy Gashadokuro. That painful ringing in your ears? It's the ethereal voices of Gashadokuro's victims, urgently whispering the location of a buried skull. It is this skull that is directing the actions of Gashadokuro. Dig up the skull and smash it to pieces. The giant skeleton will then collapse into a pile of useless bones.

Case Study 57/39g

Sightings of gargantuan monsters and demons were prevalent in 1950s Japan. No matter where you turned, it seemed another giant mutated creature was intent on destroying the country.

In response, the Japanese government published a series of Public Information Survival Guides covering what to do in the event of an attack by Rokurokubi (serpent-neck demon), Basan (giant fire-breathing chicken), Kappa (water demon), Jorōgumo (spider woman), and Gashadokuro.

The Gashadokuro guide is reproduced on the next page.

Beware!

Honored citizen.

Beware the coming of Gashadokuro!

This terrible demon of the undead once more stalks our lands.

You will know of his presence only by a painful burning sensation in the eyes, a deafening ringing in the ears, and the ground violently trembling, as if with the onset of an earthquake.

You may also hear a strange "gachi gachi" sound echoing upon the breeze as Gashadokuro grinds its teeth.

The only way to escape certain death is to run away immediately! RUN, CITIZEN! RUN!!

Children! If you are at home or in school when Gashadokuro attacks, you must hide under a table or in a closet, put your head between your knees, and say prayers to your honored ancestors that you will live to see another day!

Citizens! If you cannot escape the wrath of Gashadokuro, go happily to your death. Do not allow your last breaths of life be in anger. Otherwise your unhappy spirit may itself one day transform into Gashadokuro!

Think of your children, say a prayer to your gods and die with a smile on your face, knowing that you have saved your precious land from further dangers!

This survival guide was brought to you by the Japanese Civic Defense Authority. We are watching over you!

GASHADOKURO FACT FILE

Location: Japan, occasionally China
Appearance: A giant skeleton
Strength: It can tear down skyscrapers and snatch planes from the sky.
Weaknesses: Find its buried skull—and destroy it!
Powers: Silent movements, prodigious strength
Fear Factor: 98.7

HOW TO DEFEAT GASHADOKURO

1. Round up a thousand stray dogs.
2. Don't feed them for a week.
3. When Gashadokuro comes a-calling, let them loose. They will tear it apart and feast on its bones! (We know—genius!)
4. Don't foreget to smash its skull.

ICE GIANTS

Don't confuse these guys with the terrifying Frost Giants of Norse legend. Ice Giants are not found in frozen Nordic countries but in the wild, untamed subarctic woodland territories of the northern United States and Canada.

These guys (and ladies!) are mondo savage, and to the Algonquian-speaking Native American tribes, pose a very real threat. The creatures have a wide assortment of names—Chenoo, Rugaru, Mhwe, Windigo, Giwakwa, etc.—and there is much debate as to whether or not they are the same creature.

The term Ice Giant is itself something of a misnomer. While some do indeed reach "as tall as the clouds" and "tower above the tallest trees," others reach a mere thirty-three feet.

And here's the kicker: Not all Ice Giants are made from ice! There are as many sightings

31

of fleshy and/or hairy-furry Ice Giants as there are of oversize Frosty the Snowmen! The "ice" in this instance refers as much to the environment as it does the creature.

In northern New England, the five Wabanaki tribes (*Wabanaki* literally means "people of the dawn" or "dawnland people"—i.e. people from the east) speak in dread whisper of the terrifying creature they call Chenoo.

Metamorphosed from human to a cannibalistic giant with enormous fangs by dark shamanic enchantments, the more savage a Chenoo becomes the taller it grows. Cadaverous and gaunt from starvation, it has such insatiable hunger it will even feast on its own lips! (*Eeee-uucck!*)

The best time to track one is during the winter months, when it is on the prowl. Within its stomach lies a human-shaped lump of ice, the source of its unearthly power, and also of its downfall.

If you can trick Chenoo into vomiting up the ice (yum!), or eating enough salt that the ice inside its stomach melts, it will revert to humanoid form.

Otherwise, your best bet is to hack it into so many tiny pieces it is unable to restore itself.

Oh yes, and before hunting Chenoo, be sure to wear superpowerful ear protectors that deaden *all sound*. The scream of Chenoo will instantly kill any human who hears it! (Of course, this does mean that you can't hear it sneaking up on you, but hey, ya win some, ya lose some . . . !)

The Windigo, on the other hand, can be either iced or fur-covered. It is a gargantuan, man-eating devil spirit that preys on tribes the length and breadth of central and northeastern US.

There are many ways to transform into a Windigo, everything from a curse, dreaming about one, being bitten by one, hearing it pass by, reading about it (oh drat—too late!). But the number-one best way to become a Windigo is . . . (roll of drums, please!) . . . turn *cannibal*!

Just a nibble of human flesh is enough to turn your into a mindless, mountainous horror! And once a Windigo, your only escape from this terrible curse is . . . DEATH!!

Case Study 413/2ig

The "dream catcher" originates from the Ojibwa (Chippewa) tribe. It is made from a small willow or embroidered hoop and decorated with thread or string, beads, and feathers.

Placed at the end of the bed, the dream catcher snares all bad dreams in its web, allowing only pleasant dreams to pass through to the sleeping person. The trapped dreams disappear forever upon morning sunrise.

Here is a popular Native American folktale all about . . .

The Little Girl and the Windigo

Kanti was told by her tribal elders never to walk alone in the Wild Woods.

But, as with all young children, her inquisitiveness got the better of her.

One day, the little girl entered the woods by herself and soon became lost. Darkness fell;, frightened and tired, she lay down to sleep.

In her dream, she was awoken by heavy footfalls. Towering over the trees was a horrifying creature made from ice.

Kanti, terribly afraid, pleaded, "Please don't eat me!"

"I am not here to eat phantasms of the mind," growled the Windigo. "I have trespassed upon your dreams, as you have trespassed upon my home. When you awake, you too shall become a Windigo!"

"Noooo!" screamed Kanti. "This cannot be!"

"Whyever not?" snarled the angry Windigo.

"Because of this!" said Kanti, smiling and holding up her favorite possession.

It was a dream catcher that her grandfather, Running Through Tall Grass, had made for her.

Now it was the Windigo's turn to scream. "Nooooo!"

But it was too late. The evil spirit was trapped inside Kanti's dream!

Kanti woke up to find her mother and father beside her. Dawn was rising. "You were having a nightmare," said her mother, after she had rightly scolded Kanti for wandering off. "What was it about?"

"Strange," said Kanti, holding her dream catcher tight. "I can't remember."

Her father pointed to many sets of partially frozen giant-size footprints all around where Kanti had slept.

"Was there someone here with you last night?" he demanded, looking nervously around.

"Strange," said Kanti, as her parents hurried her out of the Wild Woods, the warm morning sunshine beaming down on her. "I can't remember that, either."

ICE GIANT FACT FILE

Location: Central and northern US, Canada

Appearance: Tall/giant, icy/furry/fleshy, take your pick

Strength: A clue—it uses fir trees as toothpicks!

Weaknesses: Silver bullet, stake through heart, decapitation, cremation

Powers: Depends on what type of Ice Giant it is. Different strokes for different folks, as they say!

Fear Factor: 52.6

THINGS TO DO WITH A CAPTURED ICE GIANT

1. Use its back as a ski slope.
2. Chill your drinks inside its cavernous mouth.
3. Set up a huge fan in front of it and use it as an air conditioner.

Meet Jiang Shi (pronounced *Chong-Shee*), definitely the strangest vampire/zombie to ever prowl the streets.

You may well laugh (go on, we'll let ya) when you find out that Jiang Shi is also known as "the hopping vampire." But beware—for Jiang Shi can kill you. Stand too close to one, and it will suck dry your very life essence!

Why is Jiang Shi such an incredible bouncing jackrabbit? Rigor mortis! Its unnatural hopping movements come from intense stiffness of the body, which is why you'll usually find it with arms outstretched. The poor dope simply can't lower them!

So what makes a Jiang Shi?

Being raised from the dead by witchcraft will do it, not being properly buried so that a stray bolt of lightning or a black and/or pregnant cat running across a coffin brings the body inside it back to un-life. (Hey, it can happen!)

Also, spirit possession by a wandering soul, a body that does not decay due to impurities in the soil, or even when a person's soul refuses to leave the body due to suicide, improper death, or simply because they were a pain in the butt in life and have no intentions of changing their attitude in death.

While some recently deceased Jiang Shi still retain a human appearance, those that have rotted underground awhile are downright gruesome.

They will have ghastly pale white skin with moss or mold growing on their flesh. Their hair is either furry green or long, white, and messy. They also sport impossibly long tongues and black, razor-sharp fingernails.

So how does one defeat such a revolting demon? In the case of Jiang Shi, the question is how does one *not*? These wackos are pathetic! Even your arthritic grandma could do it! (Check out our slammin' fact file for the full intel!)

And how's this for a laugh? Not only does a Jiang Shi have no conscious thought, it's also blind.

So if you hold your breath it doesn't even know you're there!

Case Study 249/65js

The following report was obtained under the Freedom of Information Act. It was filed by an agent of the Central Bureau of Investigation, the clandestine American government agency that investigates all paranormal sightings. Dates, names, and specific locations have been redacted to protect the innocent.

CBI

CENTRAL BUREAU OF INVESTIGATION

Rock Hardy

SPECIAL AGENT

Rock Hardy
C.B.I. Special Agent
Case No: 249/65JS
_____
_____
_____

Mutianyu, Huairou county, ▮▮▮▮

May 2, ▮▮▮▮

Reports have been coming into the Bureau of American tourists being assaulted by some undead creature while visiting the Great Wall of ▮▮▮▮.

This agent's guidebook tells him that the Great Wall in its entirety is longer than I3,I70 miles, stretching across grasslands, deserts, and mountains. Started as early as 600 BC as a series of shorter walls to stop nomadic raiders, it wasn't completed until near the end of the Ming Dynasty (I368-I644). It is the biggest structure ever built by humans.

Supposedly, something called a "Chong She" (check spelling) has been attacking tourists at various spots along the Great Wall. "I done seen this weird scary dude prowling 'round dressed like an ole-time mandarin," Mr. ▮▮▮▮ from ▮▮▮▮, revealed to me. And Mrs. ▮▮▮▮ from ▮▮▮▮ let slip that this "monster" was seen "leaping" over the Great Wall, which in this section, FYI, is twenty-five feet tall!

Early morning found this agent in the mountains, hiding furtively beneath the Great Wall. The air was thick with the scent of ginseng and jasmine. This agent glimpsed movement at the top of the wall. It was a cadaverous figure, silhouetted against the rising sun.

A C.B.I. agent never removes his sunglasses—he must protect his identity at all times—but it does mean that this agent could not see clearly. The figure could have been human, or an emaciated panda. Something long shot from its mouth, catching a passing butterfly and swallowing it whole. Gross!

Before this agent could shout, "Halt! This is the C.B.I.! You're under arrest, creep!" the figure leaped off the wall! It landed hard on top of this agent, and everything went black.

When this agent recovered, the figure had gone. No doubt it was never actually there. This agent must have accidentally tripped over a rock and cracked his head on the wall. Luckily, this agent's head is thick and no permanent damaged was suffered.

With no other evidence of actual "Chong She" activity to be found in the area, this agent concludes that such a creature does not exist. And so, as per agreement with Regional Supervisor ▮▮▮▮, this agent respectfully suggests that this case be closed, and not be presented to the relevant authorities on paranormal activities.

JIANG SHI FACT FILE

Location: China
Appearance: One seriously mugly (mondo ugly) dude!
Strength: An average strong man
Weaknesses: Easily distracted by small objects thrown at them. A six-inch piece of wood nailed to the bottom of the front door will stop it from entering. A broom. A stonemason's awl. A mirror. A peachtree branch. Also vinegar, adzuki beans, an ax, pearl rice (i.e. sticky rice), a handbell, blood from a black dog, the hoof of a black donkey, ink-stained thread, jujube seeds, fire, the call of a rooster, the intended victim holding their breath. (It seems like almost anything you like, really.)
Powers: "Hopping," sucking out your life essence.
Fear Factor: -31

THREE USES FOR A JIANG SHI

1. Use its tongue as a jump rope for your kid sister.
2. Enter it as your substitute in the school's sports day high-jump event.
3. Rent it out to the neighborhood kids to use as a really cool pogo stick.

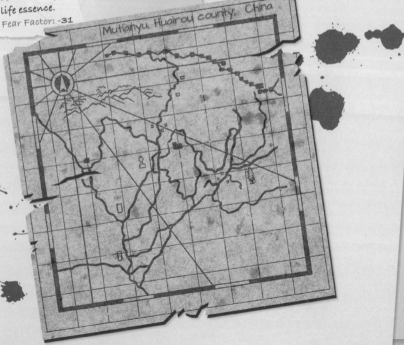

Mutianyu, Huairou county, China

Reality check: You can't claim to be legitimate monster hunter until you've hunted and captured your first mummy!

And let's face it, these guys aren't hard to recognize.

Any disease-riddled creature stalking deserts or forests wrapped in rotting bandages (or not) with its gross, dehydrated body stinking of death and decay is most likely a mummy.

Most people believe that mummies only roam the vast deserts of Egypt, and that there is little chance of being killed by one.

But they'd be WRONG!

Mummies exist on every continent of the world: Africa, Antarctica, Asia, Australia, Europe, North America, and South America. There's no escaping them!

In the cool-sounding Spirit Cave located in the desert hills of Grimes Point, seventy-five miles from Reno, Nevada, the mummified remains of an adult male were discovered that date back to 7400 BC!

(History note: The Neolithic Era dates from around 10,200 BC until 2000 BC. This was the period when humans left their caves or ended their nomadic lifestyles and began building small villages. Farming and the domestication of animals and plants also began at this time.)

And archaeologists in Chile unearthed the complete mummified body of a child that dates back to around 5050 BC.

Carbon-dated at approximately six thousand years old, the decapitated head of a mummy was found at an ancient Incan site in South America.

In Myanmar (aka Burma) in Southeast Asia, the mummified remains of at least twenty Buddhist monks can still be seen around the country. These were monks who died centuries ago, yet their bodies never decayed.

These Burmese mummies seem immune to any type of destruction. Their bodies refused to burn, even when cremated. Spooky!

(Travel note: Myanmar is bordered by China, Thailand, India, Laos, and Bangladesh. At 261,227 square miles and a population of 55,167,330, it is the second largest country in Southeast Asia. Number one? Indonesia!)

There are rumored to be over a thousand mummies in the Chinese province of Xinjiang alone!

Thankfully, the supernatural life force animating all these mummies is mostly depleted and they are no longer a threat. Yet there are still sightings of living mummies even today!

Case Study 652/77m

Here is the final entry from the journal of renowned Victorian archaeologist Sir Reginald Braithwaite, who disappeared under mysterious circumstances while excavating the lost tomb of a pharaoh in Luxor, Egypt.

Friday 13~~th~~ April 1821

While awaiting for Carruthers and the team to return with supplies, I feel an urgent need to update this log.

The workers are jittery, and causing no end of problems. They claim that this tomb is haunted, and that defilers will pay a heavy price for disturbing the resting place of the dead. Balderdash!

However, as I sit alone in this chamber, with a single lighted brazier casting dancing shadows upon these ancient walls, the air fetid with age, even I, a sophisticated man of reason, must confess to a slight unease.

And wonder why long-dead human remains wrapped in bandages make superstitious fools of us all.

The ancient Egyptians considered their pharaohs to be gods. Upon death, their followers embalmed the body and wrapped it in special linen made from the flax (linseed) plant.

They believed that a mummified body contained the spirit of the pharaoh, and would allow him to continue living in the afterlife.

The brain, eyes, lungs, liver, stomach, and intestines were removed and stored in jars. The body soaked in the chemical natron for forty days to dry it out. After this, the body was stuffed with rags and sawdust.

Wrapping a body took a full fifteen days. And twenty layers of bandages were needed to complete the gruesome task.

Finally, on the seventieth~~~~ day, the mummy was finally buried in a specially constructed sarcophagus inside a tomb.

The natives say that if you disturb a mummy's eternal rest, they will spend all eternity wandering the planet in search of bloody revenge!

Utter poppycock, of course! Silly stories to scare little children! I——But wait! I hear a strange shuffling sound approaching, as if cloth scraped on st

The journal mysteriously ends here.

41

Nonhuman Mummies

If facing off against a full-grown rampaging mummy fills you with trepidation (and sweaty armpits), consider downsizing. Human mummies are not the only threat to mankind!

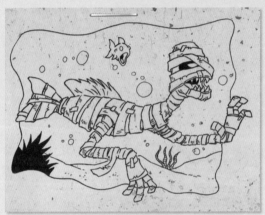

There are killer mer-mummies inhabiting the seas!

Mummified cats were big in ancient Egypt, but you'll also find stories of mummified baboons, monkeys, dogs, jackals, birds, serpents, fish, crocodiles, and even beetles that attack unwary souls in the dead of night!

MUMMY FACT FILE

Location: Worldwide
Appearance: Oh, come on! If you need a clue, you need to consider a new career!
Strength: An irate mummy has been known to smash through walls, bend iron, and even throw small vehicles!
Weaknesses: Water (except for mer-mummies, obviously!); their bodies can also be pulverized into dust
Powers: Superstrength, magic death-curse
Fear Factor: 71

HOW TO DESTROY AN EGYPTIAN MUMMY

1. Throw a jar containing the mummy's internal organs into a river.
2. Powerless to resist the attraction of its icky entrails, it will leap into the water to retrieve them, instantly dissolving to nothingness.
3. If you're hard up, do as tomb raiders did in years past, and use the leftover bandages as wrapping paper! (Eww! Better you than us!)

Pronounced *Nach*-zee-*er*-ver (say it fast, as if you're about to hack up a thick lump of phlegm, stress on the first and third syllable), the name literally means "afterward" (*nach*) "devourer" (*zehrer*).

Unlike vampires and zombies, you can't become a Nachzehrer from a bite or a scratch. Only suicide, accidental death, and, bizarrely, your name not being removed from your burial clothing will turn you into a Nachzie!

These creatures take family squabbles to a new level. While lying in its coffin, a Nachzehrer first snacks on its burial shroud—and then takes huge bites out of itself!

As it consumes its own flesh, the family member it was feuding with begins to waste away in body and soul. Their life force is literally being devoured by the Nachzehrer.

43

When bored, the Nachzehrer will claw its way out of its grave and pop over to some other recently deceased and pig out on them!

For fun, it rings the bells in a church belfry, killing everyone who hears them! Another favorite thrill-kill method is to allow its shadow to fall on someone. Instant death!

Its rotting body is covered in pus-bursting sores and *stinks* of decay, allowing it to spread deadly pestilence wherever it walks!

But its most utterly evil evilness of all? A Nachzehrer loves to sneak up behind two cows and tie their tails together! (Oooh! The beast!)

In previous centuries, with millions across Europe dropping dead from plague and disease, those lucky enough to survive blamed the epidemic on the first person in their area to die, accusing the poor sap of being a Nachzehrer.

Some would take foul revenge by digging up the body, decapitating the head, fixing the tongue so it couldn't move, and then driving a spike through its mouth to fasten the head to the ground!

History note: The Black Plague was a deadly pandemic—an epidemic of infectious diseases that occurs over a wide area. It first broke out in China in the 1330s. By 1346, it had reached Eastern Europe. From there it spread like wildfire and was especially prevalent from 1348–1550. Tens of millions died a truly agonizing death, wiping out one third of the entire European population.

How can you tell if a stiff is a Nachzehrer? First, disinter the coffin. (Yep, dig it up! After midnight is probably the best time to do this, unless you fancy getting caught and accused of grave robbing! Try explaining *that* to the cops!)

After crowbarring open the coffin lid, carefully peek inside. If the putrefying corpse is gripping the thumb of one hand in the other and one eye is wide open staring up at you, chances are it's a Nachzehrer! (And if it isn't doing this, you've messed up! In which case, we suggest you lam it—fast!)

Here's a recent blog posting from thirteen-year-old monster hunter Tobias Toombes!

A MONSTER HUNTER'S BLOG

Hallo! Guten Tag, bloggers! *Wie geht es dir? Es geht mir sehr gut, danke!* Nah, my spell-checker isn't on the fritz. I'm living in a small hamlet in northern Germany as a foreign exchange student. And guess where all the action is? The graveyard!

My "demon antenna" is tingling in overdrive the moment I arrive at this picturesque dump in the back of Teutonic Nowheresville. Bad vibes are in the air, and they aren't just coming off of my host mom's breakfast offerings of disgusting *Blutwurst* sausage! Man, those things are rank!

Investigating further, I hear whispers about strange goings-on late at night at the old church on top of the hill. *"Es ist Nachzehrer!"* one old woman hisses, nervously crossing herself as if to ward off evil spirits.

So twenty to the Midnight Hour finds Yours Truly sneaking up the hill to the church!

I quietly circle the darkened churchyard, eyeballing it for signs of Nachzehrer presence. But zip! Nada! Zilch! Or as my German teach would say, *Nichts! Nix! Null!*

That's when I hear it! A loud grunting, squealing, munching sound echoing through the graveyard! I know at once that I've found . . . a *Nachzehrer!*

When it comes to supernatural creepoids, I have an eidetic memory (total recall). Instantly, I remember my Monster Hunt Fact File entry on Nachzehrer.

One of its many undead powers is the ability to turn into a pig so it can visit family members and neighbors late at night and

45

feast on their blood! And there one is! A huge porker of a beast, fifteen hundred pounds at least, snuffling at something on the ground beside a recently dug grave!

I lift up my camera to take a snap when—OIIINNNK!—it hears me and comes a-charging! WHAAAM! Brother, am I sent flying! By the time I recover, it is gone! Dang!

The next day, my host mom is telling me about the farmer's prize hog and how it had escaped from its field late last night, and was found wandering near the church.

Seems it had been hunting for truffles that grow around the graves!

Huh! A likely story!

NACHZEHRER FACT FILE

Location: Northern Germany, northern Poland, Silesia, Bavaria

Appearance: A cadaverous undead corpse, possibly with chunks of flesh missing due to a crazed snack attack

Strength: Supernaturally powerful

Weaknesses: Placing earth under its chin, coins or stones in its mouth, or tying a handkerchief tightly around its neck will cause total paralysis. Or leave tangled nets, stockings, or knotted pieces of string inside the coffin—Nachzehrer have this mad compulsion to untie knots! And don't forget decapitation—works for us!

Powers: Cannibalistic magic, shape-shifting, plague-carrying, church bell death-peal, lethal death shadow, tying defenseless cows' tails together! (Boo!)

Fear Factor: 87.9

HOW TO ESCAPE A NACHZEHRER

SOUCOUYANT

Ever thought about a vacation in the sunny Caribbean? Well, pack your bags and grab your passport, because that's where you're heading if you want to catch yourself a Soucouyant!

Living on the outskirts of a village, the Soucouyant (aka Soucriant, Ole-Higue/Old Hag, Volant, *or* Loogaroo) is a maleficent, shape-shifting vampire witch who by day disguises herself as a sweet little old lady.

But when darkness falls, she sheds her wrinkled skin—in one piece! This is achieved by fully extending her mouth to allow the creature within to climb out.

The Soucouyant places the skin into a large black pot, jar, kettle, or mortar that has been painted in red magical symbols for protection. Whispering dread demonic incantations, she transforms into a blazing fireball!

Leaving a fiery trail across the night sky, the Soucouyant flies off in search of her latest victim. (Others may shape-shift into a skinless woman made of flames, a red hot ember, or a large burning bat, spider, or moth.)

A Soucouyant will chow down on anyone, but her favorite snacks are female kids and especially pregnant women. This allows her to take possession of the baby growing within so that she may grow up all over again. A kind of eternal un-life.

Oozing through cracks and keyholes, this hideous hag enters a home while the occupants sleep soundly. Hovering over her intended prey, she bites into the fleshy parts of their body and merrily slurps away. Her favorite spots are between the legs, toes, and fingers, under the arms and legs, and on the earlobes.

Ravenous for blood, a Soucouyant has been known to suck dry an entire village in one night!

If too much blood is taken, the victim will die (leaving the vampire witch to inhabit the skin), or they may themselves become a Soucouyant.

Those that survive are permanently changed, becoming weak and delusional for the rest of their short lives.

Are you squeamish? (A squeamish monster hunter—boy, are you in for a successful career!) If so: **DO NOT READ ANY FURTHER!!!!** Jump a paragraph and read on.

Okay: The only way to save a victim is by capturing the Soucouyant and forcing her to hack up the blood she's consumed and spit it back into the victim's mouth. (We know, *barf city*, but it has to be done!)

Catching a Soucouyant is relatively easy. All you need is a large bag of cooked rice, which you sprinkle around the village or at the village crossroads.

The Soucouyant will be compelled to pick up every single grain, one by one. Since this cannot be done before dawn, she is caught by the villagers in the morning.

To dispose of this totally evil revenant, pour either sea or cooking salt over her discarded skin. This gives her such an extreme itch attack and she can no longer bear to wear it. Without her skin, she soon shrivels up and dies. (Or re-dies, since she is already dead!)

Her only chance of survival is to take over the body of a small dying animal, such as a bat, moth, mosquito, cockroach, leech, tick, bedbug, green iguana, ocelot, luminous glowing lizard, or vampire finch.

(Yes, there *is* such a bird as the vampire finch. It's native to the Galapagos Islands in the Pacific Ocean. And they really do drink blood! Evolved from the ground finch, these small birds have extremely sharp beaks that they use to pierce the skin of the nazca booby and blue-footed booby birds, drinking the nutritious blood to supplement their diet.)

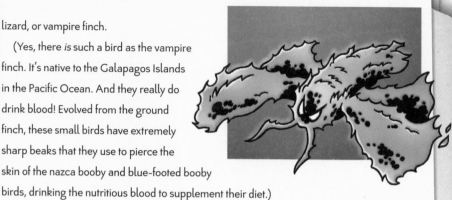

Case Study 224/77s

During our extensive investigations, we visited Port of Spain, the capital city of Trinidad and Tobago. For a donation to his favorite charity, a police officer gave us access to a recent autopsy report filed at the coroner's office.

Republic of Trinidad & Tobago

Coroner's Office, Duchess Street, Port of Spain

NAME: Xiona Coudray

AUTOPSY NO.: 77AJ/29/84B

DATE: 07-09-13

Pathologic Diagnoses

The corpse is that of a well-nourished girl of ten years old from one of the outlying villages. The body measures 4 feet 3 inches/1.3 meters and the gross weight is 55 pounds/25 kilogram.

Rigor mortis is fully developed in the muscular groups. Her body is unnaturally desiccated, her skin is shriveled and blackened, the hair has turned a premature shocking white.

Puncture marks of unknown causation are clearly visible on her right earlobe, under her right arm, and at the back of her right leg. Also between her fingers and toes. They do not appear to be insect or animal bites.

The bite holes are deep, to a depth of approximately I inch/2.5 centimeter, with dried blood specks around each circumference.

Upon opening the cadaver, I was astonished to discover a distinct lack of blood. Blood accounts for 8 percent of human body weight. A ten-year-old would normally have 4.25 pints/2 liters of blood flowing through their cardiovascular system. This child has none. She has been literally bled dry.

There are no cut marks on her body that could explain how this has been achieved. I strongly suspect that she is the sacrificial victim of an occult/ black-magic practitioner.

Isadora Slashing

Forensic Pathologist

SOUCOUYANT
FACT FILE

Location: Caribbean Islands, West Indies
Appearance: Old woman, blazing fireball/woman/animal
Strength: Human strength
Weaknesses: Rice, coarse or cooking salt sprinkled over her discarded skin
Powers: Flight, bloodsucking, size manipulation, shape-shifting, sorcery
Fear Factor: 44

WHAT TO DO WITH THE SKIN OF A SOUCOUYANT

* Stuff it full of straw and use it as a scarecrow.

Let's go hunting that bestial vampiric changeling that stalks the rain forests and forests of the Philippines—*Tiyanak*!

(Travel note: The Philippines is an archipelago of 7,107 islands in Southeast Asia, located in the western Pacific Ocean.)

Tiyanak's name comes from the Tagalog language—the language spoken as a first language by one third of the population of the Philippines and as a second language by the rest—and translated into English, *Tiyanak* means *Demon Child*!

There are a number of ways to become Tiyanak. A child who dies before being baptized, or whose mother dies before giving birth, will find their soul falling into a chamber at the edge of hell known as limbo, where they will be transformed into this most diabolic monstrosity.

Tiyanak may also be the offspring of a demon and a human mother. Or a Tiyanak may abduct a child from its crib and carry it away. Once bitten, this child shall die and become Tiyanak!

Whatever its origins, when it comes back to un-life it is out for bloody revenge!

Lurking deep inside the jungle foliage waiting to pounce, Tiyanak (aka Impakto) has the ability to mimic the cries of a newborn baby in distress, thus drawing a concerned passerby to its lair. It may also take the form of a specific child that it has stolen and murdered.

Human instinct is to pick up and comfort an abandoned infant. Bad move, dude! At that instant, Tiyanak reverts to its true form and attacks!

The victim dies either by being bitten on the neck by its powerful fangs and sucked dry of blood, or else slashed to death by Tiyanak's razor-sharp claws!

Tiyanak's shape-shifting abilities allow it to transform into a large black bird or a nut-brown dwarf with a large nose, large angry eyes, a wide mouth (all the better to eat you with!), and a sharp voice.

Other times the murderous munchkin will become a wrinkled little old man with a long beard and moustache and a flat nose. In this form, one leg is shorter than the other, so Tiyanak must resort to leaping onto its prey.

When Tiyanak is in a more playful mood, it may lead an unwary traveler deep into the rain forest with its toddler cries until the person is completely lost and disorientated and unable to find a way back out again.

Threatened on all sides by hungry jungle animals and poisonous reptiles and insects, the traveler eventually goes mad or starves to death!

Case Study 0057/18t

Neela Nightshade, ace reporter for the Weekly
World Examiner, recently filed this report.

Demon Child Found in Forest

Weekly World Examiner Exclusive

PALAWAN ISLAND, Philippines, July 29

The largest island of the Palawan province, Palawan Island is a tropical
paradise. With its bounteous wildlife, white sandy beaches, fertile mountain
jungles, and stunning seascapes and landscapes, it is the most biodiverse
island in the Philippines.

Sadly, like all other rain forests globally, this one is facing extinction by
deforestation. A hundred years ago, 70 percent of the Philippines was covered
in verdant rain forest. Now it is less than 7 percent!

If this trend continues, in fifteen to twenty years there will be no rain
forest left. Of the roughly 14,500 species of animals and plants living in
these rainforests, more than 3,600 are endemic to the Philippines. They exist
nowhere else. When the rain forests are gone, so too will be all this amazing
fauna and flora.

As this reporter has stated before, humans are the scariest "monsters" of
them all!

But today, the hunter becomes the hunted. The savage becomes . . . the
savaged!

Sent to investigate sightings of the supernatural entity known as Tiyanak,
I am traveling into the rain forest with my guide——an experienced hunter.

"Y'all ain't got no need t'worry, l'il Missy," grunts Brutus Redneck
condescendingly, lovingly caressing his *KRISS Super V* submachine gun.
"When ole Brutus finds this dumb beastie, ole Brutus's weapon will plumb shed

53

him to itsy-bitsy pieces! Yee-haaa!"

That's when we both hear a high-pitched wailing deep within the foliage!
"Waaa-aaah! Waaa-aaah!"

The plaintive cry of an infant in distress sends cold tendrils of fear washing over me. I am almost convinced that there is a helpless baby lost in the forest!

My maternal instinct is to rush in and find the poor child, but reason holds me back. What, I ask myself, is a baby doing alone in the jungle?!

Reasoning, unfortunately, is not one of Brutus's strong points.

"Waaa-hoooo!" he yelps excitedly, bulldozing his way into the forest darkness and disappearing from view. "Wait there, missy! 'Cause ol' Brutus gonna plumb bag himself the Devil's offspring! Yeee-haaaa!"

Mouth dry, I count the seconds with my pounding heart. The sound of rapid machine-gun fire makes me flinch! As does what follows. The heart-wrenching death-screams of Brutus Redneck himself! **"Yaaaaa-aaaaah!"**

Then silence descends upon the forest.

Suddenly, this hideous shape flies out from the undergrowth, skimming over my head! A deformed child, all fangs and claws, dripping fresh blood!

I automatically snap off a shot! And then I run! Run!! RUN!!! Until I am once again safely back on the outskirts of civilization!

TIYANAK FACT FILE

Location: Republic of the Philippines
Appearance: Infant, black bird, wizened old man, dwarf
Strength: Inhumanly strong
Weaknesses: Inside-out clothes (slightly bizarre, but let's face it, with Tiyanak about to strike, who has time to change their clothes?! Your underwear, maybe . . . you might need to . . .). Loud/rude noises. Rosary beads. Garlic (chew on a garlic bulb before the hunt—your stinky breath may save your life! It may also cost you all your friends, but what the heck!)
Powers: Shape-shifting, mimicry, flight, super leaps, bloodsucking, razor-sharp claws
Fear Factor: 61.5

WHAT TO DO WITH A "DWARF" TIYANAK

COVER IT IN CONCRETE AND USE AS A GARDEN GNOME!

Vampires have been scaring the sweet bejeebers out of good, honest folk and supping their blood as an aperitif ever since humans first learned how to daub childish pictures onto cave walls using icky red animal fluids.

The Mesopotamians, Phoenicians, and ancient Greeks and Romans all had run-ins with these foul bloodsuckers!

Vampires were first mentioned thousands of years ago, in stories written in Sanskrit, the language of ancient India and arguably one of the oldest known languages in the world.

The Baital Pachisi—otherwise known as *Vikram & the Vampire*—was a series of twenty-five short stories that were later translated for a wider audience by the scholar Bhavabhuti around AD 730.

Vikram's vampire was more of a trickster than one with evil intent. Yet only three centuries later, in 1047, a document appeared referring to a Russian prince as *Upir*, which is short for *Upir Lichy* or *Wicked Vampire*!

So if you think that vampires only started appearing after the publication of British writer James Malcolm Rymer's *Varney the Vampire: or, the Feast of Blood* published in 1847, think again! (This story saw print exactly fifty years before Bram Stoker's *Dracula*!)

Forget the young, handsome Hollywood depiction of vampires. In their true forms, these creatures are truly vile and disgusting abominations.

Their bodies are bloated from the buildup of gases while they were interred for three days in their coffin, their skin dark or purplish and decomposing. And they smell like you would imagine a rotting corpse to smell—*ultra foul*!

Beware! Vampires are shape-shifters, and can disguise their gross-out appearance to look almost human, take on an animal guise, or even turn *invisible*!

Chinese and Slavic people believed that any animal, but particularly a cat or dog, leaping over a fresh corpse would bring it back to undead life. In some cultures, not placing a scythe or sickle near a new grave, or a coin in a corpse's mouth, or even forgetting to pour boiling water onto a corpse's wound, meant that it would soon be back to feed—on *you*!

In Eastern Europe, dying from the bite of a vampire results in your undead return three days hence, unless some kind soul thrusts a wooden stake through your heart and chops off your head! (Gruesome, but highly effective!)

Case Study 0057/18t

A Dhampir in Balkan folklore is the child born of a vampire and a human woman. These children possess similar powers to vampires, but without the weaknesses. Many Dhampir hu~ and kill vampires.

We recently unearthed a secret scrapbook kept by a young Dhampir, detailing the stalkin~ of her vampiric father. The following is just a sample from this amazing discovery:

VAMPIRE AT LARGE?

January 17—Romania. Tracked Father to a small village sixteen kilometers from Brasov. Three villagers found dead in past week with puncture wounds on neck.

January 20—Staked out village graveyard. Thirteen below. The days are dark and bitter, mirroring my heart. The trees are covered in ice. Midnight, and a mist forms around a recently dug grave.

The mist transforms into Father. "Rise, my undead minion! Rise!" he incants. The earth on top of the grave begins to move and a decomposing hand thrusts up from out of the ground!

"Father! Desist!" I cry, emerging from the shadows, crucifix in hand.

He turns, hissing in fury, but stays his hand. He could never harm me.

"Another time, daughter," he chuckles softly, turning swiftly into a bat and flying away.

I wait for Father's newly awoken vampire soldier to rise from beneath the glistening soil. I pick up my ax, then swing it hard and chop off his head!

Father, this I promise—you will be next!

VAMPIRE FACT FILE

Location: Worldwide

Appearance: Anything they want, but usually human

Strength: Some are not much stronger than a normal human. Others possess super-normal strength. Their strength increases the longer they un-live.

Weaknesses: Forget sunlight; that's a myth. Vampires prefer the night, but only so that they can hunt prey without interference. However, for creatures with such a fearsome rep, they are susceptible to a whole catalogue of threats: garlic, wild rose, hawthorn, oak, ash, mustard seed, a crucifix or rosary, holy water, steel, iron, mirrors, river and sea water, and some even fear bricks and lemons! It all depends upon the type of vampire you're hunting. Choose the wrong apotropaic object—something that wards off evil—and you'll very soon be a vampire's dinner!

Powers: Immortality. Shape-shifting. Flight. Superstrength. Hypnotism. Control of animals. Misting and vaporizing. Weather control. Invisibility. Command of the dead.

Fear Factor: If we were marking merely on Image Factor alone, definitely 100; however, even though vampires are mega-fearsome, they can be killed.

Fear Factor: 86.3

5 USES FOR A VAMPIRE
(ONCE YOU'VE CAUGHT ONE)

1. Make it change into a small bat and hide it in your sister's bedroom!
2. Hypnotize your mom to let you stay up late during the school week!
3. Use its fangs as a bottle opener to pull the caps off your soda!
4. Transform to wolf form to chase off next door neighbor's cat and stop it from pooping in the garden!
5. Turn into an impenetrable mist to close all schools in your area for the day!

Vampires-101

1) Never seen in Daylight
2) Scared of Crosses
3) No Reflection
4) Turn into b

A Zombie is a dead human brought back to un-life through the power of witchcraft!

This type of dark sorcery is known to its followers variously as *vodun* (in Africa), *vodou* (in Haiti), and in the swamplands Louisiana it's called voodoo.

Each type of black magic is similar in its practices, but there are some distinct differences. For example, Louisiana voodoo (sometimes referred to as New Orleans voodoo) concentrates more on a chosen Voodoo Queen and the use of voodoo dolls and gris-gris (magic talismans) in its ceremonies.

History note: Zombies are believed to have first been described in ancient Egyptian hieroglyphics around 3000 BC. This ancient writing form used symbols to represent objects and ideas. It dates back to either 3300 or 3200 BC. The Egyptians used hieroglyphics (literally

59

ZOMBIES

translated as the "sacred carving") for the next 3,500 years.

To create a Zombie, a bokor—voodoo sorcerer—casts a spell to reanimate a dead body. This Zombie has no will of its own. It is under the complete control of the bokor, who usually uses it to exact bloody revenge on his or her most hated enemies.

Depending upon the age of the dead person, a Zombie may still have the appearance of the living, with only a blank expression, stiff movements, and shambling gait revealing them to be one of the Undead.

Zombie bodies that have been buried awhile will have decaying, peeling flesh, and emaciated or even skeletal frames. All Zombies give off a strong, musty smell.

Once resurrected to a pitiful un-life, the Zombie can last for decades, until the bokor controlling it dies. Then it automatically returns to the grave from whence it came.

If bitten by a Zombie, it will take you some days to actually die. Your brain slowly disintegrates, and your body transform into Zombie state. The bad news? There's no known antidote!

Still, at least you've got time to pig out on your favorite junk food, and you won't have to worry about it being bad for your health! ●

The following documents were obtained under the Freedom of Information Act.

The first is a letter from a concerned citizen to the Central Bureau of Investigation, the clandestine American government agency that investigates all paranormal sightings.

The second is a report filed by an agent of the C.B.I. Dates, names, and specific locations have been redacted to protect the innocent.

Deer Govermint Man

Me'n me best pal Zeke, wee wuz out by the bayou hopin' to huntt sum lil criters wiv our shotguns whens wee saw this big galoot cumin' out of them bushes. Hee wuz big like wiv yello skin n' the blakkest eyes you ever dun seen. Hee growlled loudlee at us bfore disapeeren back intoo the unnderrgroth. Wee rekonn y'all should proply ~~envissttigrate~~ ~~invicttigat~~ look into it.

Yur good pal, Cletus Hogtrotter

Rock Hardy
C.B.I. Special Agent
‾‾

Case No: 413/37Z ‾‾‾‾‾‾‾‾ ‾ ‾‾‾‾‾‾‾‾‾‾‾‾‾‾‾‾‾‾

On ▮▮▮▮▮ May 10, ▮▮▮ at approximately 16:22 hours, this agent responded to a possible "Zombie" sighting around the swamps and bayous of New Orleans Louisiana.

Citizens reported sighting a terrifying "creature" whose strange appearance includes black, soulless eyes and putrid green skin.

This agent tracked the suspected "Zombie" to the outskirts of the bayou. He photographed various-size footprints, and discovered the remains of a dead alligator, eviscerated from throat to tail. Its internal organs, having been violently ripped out, lay partially eaten on the ground.

Chicken bones lay close by. "That be a sure sign of a Satanic Voodoo Queen, that be"—claimed old Mrs. ▮▮▮▮▮▮▮, This agent has a much simpler answer. The gator ate the chicken, and a bigger gator then attacked and killed it.

With darkness falling and night mists rising, and finding no other clues, this agent began heading out of the bayou. Suddenly, this agent received a sharp blow on the back of the head and fell almost insensible to the ground.

His vision impaired by this cowardly attack, this agent believed he saw a huge, dark, lumbering object appear in front of him. The object gave off a pitiful moan of despair before shuffling back into the darkness. This agent then lost consciousness.

Upon awakening, this agent discovered a large tree branch lying beside him. No doubt this had broken free from a tree and struck this agent on the head, causing momentary hallucinations, both visual and auditory.

Therefore, with no other evidence of actual "Zombie" activity to be found in the area, and per agreement with Regional Supervisor ████████, this agent respectfully suggests that this case be closed, and not be presented to the relevant authorities on paranormal activities.

ZOMBIE FACT FILE

Location: West Africa, Central Africa, the West Indies, the Caribbean, Brazil, Haiti, the Dominican Republic, and Cuba, and in the swamplands of New Orleans, Louisiana

Appearance: Mugly, stinky, and dumb-looking!

Strength: Depends on how strong they were in life. A puny Zombie isn't going to be much of a threat! And if they are—shame on you!

Weaknesses: Stupidity; slowness; fire

Powers: The dreaded Zombie-bite!

Fear Factor: Well, they look gruesome, but come on! These guys are about as scary as your math teacher! (Unless your math teacher is really scary, that is!)

Fear Factor: 23

HOW TO TRAP A ZOMBIE

1. Dig a deep pit. Cover it with branches or straw.
2. When the Zombie chases you, run around the pit.
3. Being thick as a brick, the Zombie will shamble across the pit and fall in.
4. It will now spend the rest of eternity walking around in circles, not realizing that it can just climb out again!

BAYKOK

Location: Forests of the Great Lakes, Canada
Appearance: Emaciated skeleton-like figure, translucent desiccated skin, skull head, red points for eyes or black, soulless eyes
Strength: Horrifying!
Weaknesses: Smashing Baykok into tiny bone shards and then cremating. (Beware: If even one sliver survives, the Baykok will recreate itself and come looking for bloody vengeance!)
Powers: Paralyzing prey with invisible arrows; beating prey to death with a club. After paralyzing or killing its victim, this demon slices open its prey's stomach and munches on its fresh, juicy liver. (Only attacks warriors of the Chippewa nation.)
Fear Factor: 48

BLOODY MARY

Location: United Kingdom, United States
Appearance: Rotting corpse, witch, or ghost, covered in blood
Strength: Frightening!
Weaknesses: Turning mirror to face the wall, smashing mirror (but then risking seven years bad luck . . . hey, ho—easy come, easy go!)
Powers: Bloody Mary is summoned by standing in a darkened bathroom at night, holding a lighted candle, and staring at a mirror, repeatedly chanting loudly, "Bloody Mary! Bloody Mary! Bloody Mary!" (You may also need to spin around with each incantation.) Mary will then appear in the mirror to scream and curse at you, rip out your eyeballs, tear out your tongue, horribly scar your face with her razor-talons, claw you to death, strangle you, drink your blood, drive you insane, kill you stone dead, steal your soul, or pull you into the mirror so that you are trapped therein with Bloody Mary for all eternity!
Fear Factor: 94.5

CRAQUEHHE

Location: **France**

Appearance: **Rotting corpse with bloated maggots, worms, and other insects crawling out from its hair, face, hands, feet, and torso. Sunken red eyes, yellowish-white translucent skin, long greasy hair matted with grave dirt.**

Strength: **Prodigious**

Weaknesses: **Crucifix, fire, decapitation. [If the body is not completely cremated, it will be resurrected.]**

Powers: **One of the most powerful and savage of European revenants, the daddy of all zombies. Shambles along slowly to fool its victims into thinking they can escape, and then pounces with breathtaking speed. Prefers both eating the flesh and drinking the blood of its prey. Carries deadly diseases. Can infect an entire cemetery with its evil in order to bring forth an army of Undead brethren. Impervious to pain. Chop off its head or cut it in half and it will continue to hunt you down.**

Fear Factor: **86**

EL CUCO

Location: **Spain, Portugal, Brazil, Argentina, Chile**

Appearance: **Human form with pumpkin/dragon/alligator head. It's a shape-shifter, so basically whatever it feels like.**

Strength: **Read the above and hazard your own guess!**

Weaknesses: **So far in our investigations, we haven't found any!**

Powers: **Hides in closets and under the bed, devouring disobedient children, especially those who won't go to sleep. An early seventeenth-century Spanish nursery rhyme goes:**
Duérmete niño, duérmete ya . . . (Sleep child, sleep now . . .)
Que viene el Cuco y te comerá. (Or else the Cuco will come and eat you.) **So, no pressure!**

Fear Factor: **If you're a naughty kid, 98.8 at the very least (that and a very wet bed!)**

GHOUL

Location: Middle East, Africa, Asia
Appearance: Cadaverous human, desiccated skin, bulging yellow eyes with glazed demeanor, large mouth with tiny razor-sharp teeth, clawed hands, lanky arms, skin light blue or gray
Strength: Immense
Weaknesses: Low intelligence, incapable of speech. Can be destroyed by sunlight, fire, electrocution, acid bath, massive explosion, decapitation
Powers: Revived nocturnal corpse that hides out in cemeteries, abandoned places, or in the desert. Cowardly; prefers to hunt in packs. Attacks the living, drinks their blood, and devours them. Eats fresh corpses, taking on their form. Can shape-shift into any animal. Immortal, impervious to pain, three times as agile and fast as when alive; regenerative powers, heightened night vision and sense of smell (can smell human flesh—dead or alive—up to 1 mile).
Fear Factor: 73.1

GJENGANGER

Location: Scandinavia
Appearance: Rotting corpse
Strength: A bit feeble
Weaknesses: Carrying the coffin around a church three times, wearing a crucifix, carving an inscription inside the coffin that faces the body
Powers: Spreads death-dealing disease by pinching the victim very hard on the arm
Fear Factor: 1.2

KUDLAK

Location: Croatia, Slovenia
Appearance: Animal form (alive); Vampire (dead)
Strength: Supernatural
Weaknesses: Hawthorn stake through the heart, tendon slashed below the knee before burial
Powers: Someone born with a red or dark caul on their head may become a Kudlak. (A caul is a portion of the amniotic sac that may still cling to a baby's head after birth.) When alive, their soul can leave the body at night in animal form and fly through villages attacking people; the Kudlak can also perform evil magic spells. When dead, the person becomes an undead vampire, sucking blood and sowing pestilence and misfortune.
Fear Factor: 36

MANANANGGAL

Location: The Visayan region of the Republic of the Philippines, notably the western provinces of Antique, Capiz, and Iloilo
Appearance: By day, old but beautiful woman; by night, wild-eyed and long-haired hag.
Strength: Average
Weaknesses: Sunlight, garlic, vinegar, onion, spices, salt, dagger, tail of a stingray fashioned into a whip, ash, raw rice, or burning rubber. If the bottom half of its torso can be found and the flesh sprinkled with ash, salt, or garlic, the Manananggal cannot rejoin and will perish at dawn.
Powers: Ability to separate its upper torso from the lower, giant bat wings to fly, extendable and flexible needle-fine hollow tongue with razor-sharp point that pierces victim's skin to suck out their blood.
Fear Factor: 91.9

MULLO

Location: The nomadic Romani (Gypsy) people of Europe and the US

Appearance: Recently dead male (Mullo) or female (Muli) human with only three or four fingers, scaly skin, and eyes "alight with fire"

Strength: Strong vampire

Weaknesses: Drive iron or steel needles through its heart and place pieces of steel in its mouth, over its eyes, in its ears, and between its fingers. Pour boiling water over it. Decapitation. Thrust a hawthorn stake through the legs to stop it from walking. Place a sprig of hawthorn in its socks.

Powers: Soul-sucking (as opposed to the usual bloodsucking), bad-luck curse. (Usually a revenge thing for a relative who has caused its death or kept the deceased's property or did not observe proper death rites. Traditionally, Romani people and their belongings are always cremated together.)

Fear Factor: 11

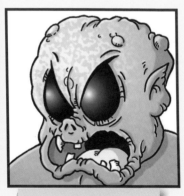

MYLING

Location: Scandinavia

Appearance: Enormous and grotesque baby form

Strength: Ghastly strength and fury

Weaknesses: Water and iron

Powers: Beginning as an unwanted baby abandoned in woods or forest and left to die, its unbaptized soul cannot rest. The body is reanimated and cursed to roam the Earth. The Myling will leap onto the back of unwary travelers and demand to be carried to a graveyard to receive proper burial. It multiplies its weight with each step, until the victim either sinks into the ground or is crushed to death. If it does not reach a graveyard, it will fly into a murderous howling rage. It may also haunt the parents who abandoned it until they commit suicide. Other powers: invisibility; shape-shifting into a snowy owl, a black dog, or curl of smoke. In all its guises, it can grow to the size of a barn. A glimpse of a Myling can fatally paralyze a human.

Fear Factor: 63.6

NELAPSI

Location: **Slovakia**

Appearance: **Lean, muscular build, piercing red eyes, needle-thin fangs and teeth, long greasy hair, razor-sharp talons on hands and feet. Possesses two hearts. May appear in tattered clothes or burial shroud, or even stark naked!**

Strength: **Über-supernatural**

Weaknesses: **Poppy and millet seeds, garlic, hat pin, iron wedge, stake made from hawthorn, blackthorn, or oak, fire, decapitation, snow-white horse walking across its grave**

Powers: **The most vicious, powerful and psychotic of all vampires, Nelapsi has a 24/7 insatiable bloodlust. It can butcher an entire village in a single night! A simple glare from its burning red eyes will kill. Anthropophagous (a cannibal), Nelapsi either crushes its victim in a bone-breaking clinch before tearing off parts of the body to chow down on, or rips the victim to shreds with its teeth before drinking the body dry of blood. Its strength, speed, endurance, and agility are intense. Nelapsi's favorite hobby is torturing its victim for endless weeks, driving them insane, before killing and eating them. (Or eating and then killing them, depending on what day of the week it is.) It will attack both humans and animals with equal glee. Carries a horrific plague virus that kills everyone for miles around.**

Fear Factor: **97.6**

STRIGOI

Location: **Romania, Croatia, Serbia**

Appearance: **Usually a woman, but can be male. Red hair, blue eyes, and two hearts. Can turn into an animal (usually a dog, frog, flea, or bedbug) or a small spark of light.**

Strength: **If you are farm crops or an animal, be afraid, be very afraid!**

Weaknesses: **Bury a bottle of whiskey with the corpse. After it pops out for its nightly haunt, it will get so drunk it will forget where it's buried! Exhume the body, cut out its hearts, and slice it in two; hammer a nail through its forehead. Finally, place the body back in its grave facedown.**

Powers: **Steals the vitality and/or life force of its neighbor's animals and crops. Invisibility.**

Fear Factor: **14**

WATER BEASTS

What would an ocean be without a monster lurking in the dark?

—Werner Herzog

—German film director (1942– present)

One of the most important of all the sciences that a newbie monster hunter should study is cryptozoology. The term *cryptozoology* comes from the ancient Greek words (yep, those guys again) *kryptos*, meaning hidden, plus *zoology*, the study of animals and encompasses all creatures where there is little actual "proof" that they exist. This includes such "celebs" as the Loch Ness Monster, the Yeti, and the Mongolian Death Worm!

The tag was coined by Scottish biologist, writer, explorer, adventurer, and all-round macho man Ivan T. Sanderson (1911–1973) who was intrigued by both the numerous sightings of strange creatures and in paranormal events.

Cryptid—the scientific name for the unexplained beasts that we track down—was first used by scientist John E. Wall in 1983 when writing to the International Society of Cryptozoology newsletter. While this Society closed its doors in 1998, there is now the International Cryptozoological Society, which offers unofficial cryptozoology merit badges to the Boy Scouts of America! (Cool!)

So how do we know that there are strange and bizarre life forms still to be discovered?

Astonishingly, although more than two million species of fauna and flora—animals and plants to you and us—have been identified, many of whom now face extinction thanks to humans and our innate greed and thoughtlessness, scientists guesstimate that there are anywhere from five million to a hundred million more species yet to be discovered!

So the chances of there being monstrous aquatic creatures roaming the world is pretty high, especially when we consider that only a miserly 1 percent of the seafloor has so far been explored, and that there are untold hundreds of thousands of lakes and rivers across the planet.

And we have some seriously gnarly fiends just waiting to wrap their slimy tentacles around you. Aside from the classic river serpents, there's also the giant Wuhan Toads of China! Party animal Tarasque from France, who loves to munch on fresh human flesh! Japan's mountain-size Umibōzu! From the Bahamas, Lusca, the vicious half-shark/half-octopi hybrid! Vodianoi, the green-bearded Slavic Undead spirits whose bite will turn you into an aquatic Zombie! (No kidding!)

The cute-but-deadly Japanese Kappa! The Mediterranean's beautiful but deadly Sirens! Dingonek! Mamlambo! Ningyo! Dobhar-Chú! Inkanyamba! Aspidochelone! Llamhigyn y Dwr! And even some beasties whose names we can pronounce! These guys need to be seen to be believed!

So put on your flippers and diving mask, grab your fishing net, and come take a dip with us into the deep, dark, dangerous, and totally zowsers amphibious universe of the Water Beasts!

ASPIDOCHELONE

Okay, all you hard-core monster hunters, the first nautical nightmare we'll be hunting is . . . a *turtle*!

"Ooooh!" we hear you sarcastically squeal. "That is, like, sooo scary, dude!" Well, actually, smarty-pants, this one is, because it's the size of *an island*!

This overgrown aquatic tortoise is old. Like *ancient*! He's first mentioned in the *Physiologus*, a manuscript written sometime around AD 200 in Alexandria, capital city of Egypt, from its founding by Alexander the Great in 331 BC until AD 641. Many of the stories in the book are said to date back much further; some are thought to have been written by Aristotle or Solomon!

Old Shellback was also featured in Roman naturalist and philosopher Pliny the Elder's encyclopedia *Naturalis Historia* (published circa AD 77–79), then in the *Kitab al-Hayawan* (*Book of Animals*) by ninth century Arabic author al-Jāhiz (real name Abu Uthman Amr ibn Bahr al-Kinani al-Fuqaimi al-Basri).

His celeb status increased tenfold with an appearance in the 1220 Anglo-Saxon *Bestiary* and yet again in Zakariya' ibn Muhammad al-Qazwini's best-selling book, *Marvels of Things Created and Miraculous Aspects of Things Existing.* (al-Qazwini was an Arab scholar, astronomer, physician, geographer, and—we kid you not—science fiction writer who died in 1283.)

The monster guest-starred in the first voyage of Sinbad the Sailor in *The Book of One Thousand and One* Nights and in English poet John Milton's book *Paradise Lost* (published in 1667). This Not-So-Teenage-Mutant-Turtle has more followers than most people have on Facebook!

In some cultures, Aspidochelone (aka Aspidodeleone, Asp-Turtle, Zaratan, Fastitocalon, and Balain) is considered a pal of Satan himself. Some claim he's the biblical "whale" that swallowed Jonah. Medieval Christians often depicted his opened jaws as the entrance to the mouth of hell!

Aspidochelone

He's part turtle, part snake, which is where the *asp* connotation comes in. In ancient Greek, *aspis* means asp or shield and *chelone* means tortoise. But all agree that he swims around the planet deceiving sailors into thinking he's a desert island of golden sand and lush palm trees.

Once the sailors are safely on "land," Aspidochelone pops his head out of the water, cackles evilly, and slowly sinks beneath the waters, dragging the unfortunate sailors down with him!

Case Study 101/43a

During our search for Aspidochelone, we came across a short story that was left out of *The Book of One Thousand and One Nights*!

The King and the Slave

There was once a seafaring king from a Persian city who delighted in treating his slaves in a harsh and haughty way.

When he put to sea on his latest voyage, the king was of foul temper and mean-spirited. During a spell of rough weather, a slave spilled his drink. The furious king did whip the miserable wretch to within an inch of his life.

Cried the man most piteously, "Spare me so God may spare thee, O King!" but the king spurned his pleas and did deal with him most cruelly.

He bade the other slaves to strip the man, bind him, and attach heavy weights to his legs. "Oh vilest and meanest and cruelest of kings," spoke the man angrily, knowing that his day of judgment was at hand. "By Allah the Merciful, I shall make vengeance upon thee!"

Whereupon the king ordered the man be thrown out into the sea, and thus he disappeared beneath the Stygian waters.

That night, there arose the most terrible of tempest. It mightily crushed the ship of the cruel king. All were lost, save one.

"Oh Thou that answered my prayers," wept the king, holding tight to the shattered remains of his ship to keep from drowning. "Help me in mine hour of need."

With dawn's early light, the king's eyes set upon an island, and thereby made landing.

"I am saved!" bellowed the king to the Heavens. "Now all who knoweth mine story will declare that I be the mightiest king of them all!"

"Thou be neither mighty nor saved," said a voice the king instantly recognized. He looked down to see on the sandy shore the face of the slave he had so recently murdered.

"Nay! 'Tis not possible!" cried the king, shrinking back fearfully. "It be a devil's demon come to haunt me!"

Quoth the face, "Or thy conscience come to prick thee."

At that, the island began to violently shake. From one end there appeared the giant tail of an asp, at the other, the head of a turtle.

"Aspidochelone!" cried the king in utmost terror. In desperation, he did try to escape from this island, but the shifting sands held fast his feet.

Sobbed he pitifully, falling to his knees in prayer, "Oh slave, I beseech thee! Have mercy upon me!"

"Didst thou show me mercy?" said the slave, as the island began to sink beneath the waves. "I thinketh not, Oh Great King. I thinketh not."

ASPIDOCHELONE FACT FILE

Location: Mediterranean Sea, Pacific and Indian Oceans
Appearance: Giant turtle, turtle/snake combo, giant fish or whale
Strength: Definitely not a wimp!
Weaknesses: Um, anyone got a spare nuke we could borrow?
Powers: Cunning disguise
Fear Factor: 96.3

WHAT TO DO WITH ASPIDOCHELONE

(Once you've caught him.)
1. Sell him to an A-list celebrity so they can hide from the paparazzi.
2. Rent him out to a megalomaniac world-conquering super-villain to use as a secret base (and thereby share his ill-gotten gains!).
3. Use him as a floating prison for all the other monsters you catch!

ПОБЕДА!

There are many reasons why the Allies won World War II.

From 1939 until 1945 the stouthearted British, fighting alongside forces from France, Poland, Canada, Australia, New Zealand, India, South Africa, and China among others, battled tirelessly against the tyrannical Axis nations of Germany, Italy, and Japan.

The brave citizens of the Soviet Union fought a desperate and bloody war to throw the German invaders and their allies out of Russia, with a loss of almost twenty-four million lives.

And of course America helped to kick Axis butt when she entered the war in 1941, after a sneak attack by Japanese forces on the US naval base at Pearl Harbor on December 7.

However, unknown to most war historians, the Soviet Union had a helping hand in their struggle against the jackbooted Nazis thugs. A terrifying secret weapon so powerful it could have brought an end to the war all by itself.

Its name—the *Brosno Dragon*!

This horrifying cryptid (aka Brosnya) resides in Lake Brosno near Andreapol, two hundred and fifty miles northwest of Moscow.

Rising up to a height of sixteen feet, the Brosno Dragon is a bioluminescent monstrosity (It glows, especially in the dark! Neat!) that appears each evening to menace nearby villages. It overturns boats and eats anyone silly enough to doggy-paddle in the lake.

At least one German pilot met a grisly end when he flew across the lake to attack the Russian capital. Rearing up from the depths, the Brosno Dragon snatched the plane out of the sky!

Fighting the Nazis isn't the first time Brosnie has defended the motherland.

It also attacked both the Vikings (ninth through eleventh centuries) and the Tartar-Mongol horde of Batu Khan (Genghis Khan's grandson) when they invaded in 1237–1240.

In 2002, monster hunters from the Kosmopoisk research association went on an expedition to hunt down this elusive creature.

A huge jelly-like mass the size of a school bus was detected sixteen feet from the bottom of the lake. Exploding a low capacity depth charge, the scientists watched their sonar screen in astonishment as the object swam off!

Near the Siberian lake of Sestakovo, paleontologists have found the bones of a prehistoric creature, similar to the descriptions of the Brosno Dragon.

Due to its shape and mammal-like teeth, it is believed that Brosnie comes from the family known as pre-mammalian synapsids (vertebrates that possess skulls with one opening behind the eye socket and one fused temporal arch) that first appeared over 320 million years ago (the late Carboniferous period) and totally owned the Permian and early Triassic periods.

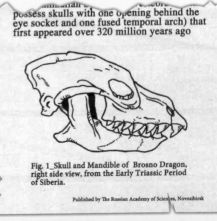

possess skulls with one opening behind the eye socket and one fused temporal arch) that first appeared over 320 million years ago

Fig. 1_Skull and Mandible of Brosno Dragon, right side view, from the Early Triassic Period of Siberia.

Published by The Russian Academy of Sciences, Novosibirsk

Case Study 611/4bd

We hired famed Romani psychic Madame Aysi Kleerlee to make contact with the spirit of World War II Soviet Union premier, mass murderer, and all-around evil dictator Joseph Stalin to discuss his use of the Brosno Dragon against his enemies.

Transcript from a Madame Aysi Kleerlee direct-voice communication:

A Séance with Stalin

Date: March 20

Sitters: John Gatehouse, Dave Windett

Communicators: Joseph Stalin

KLEERLEE: (calling) Halloooo! Is there anyone there?

(Silence, then voice fades in)

STALIN: (addressing another spirit) . . . that is all very well, Genghis, but when we conquer Purgatory we must send out our death squads to eradicate any rebel spirits . . .

KLEERLEE: (excited) Premier Stalin! You're coming through perfectly!

STALIN: (growls) Who is this? How did you get in here?! Guards! Guards!

KLEERLEE: I'm speaking from the other side . . .

STALIN: The other side of what? The Berlin Wall?! No, that was torn down in 1989 . . . (sad) I get confused sometimes . . . so confused . . . time is ethereal over here . . . you grasp it, and then it is gone . . . gone . . .

KLEERLEE: I'm a friend, Joe . . .

STALIN: (chuckles) AH! A Communist! Good! Good! The Devil's on my side, you know. He's a good Bolshevik. We get on well together; he and I . . . like old friends . . . (unintelligible mumblings) . . .

KLEERLEE: Speak up, Joe . . . I can't quite hear you . . .

STALIN: (roars) I AM JOSEPH VISSARIONOVICH STALIN!!! NO ONE TELLS ME WHAT TO DO!!! I will have you shot! Guards! Guards!

KLEERLEE: I-I didn't mean to offend . . . thank you for talking to me . . .

STALIN: (laughs) Ha! Gratitude is a sickness suffered by dogs!

KLEERLEE: Hmm, quite. So Joe, I want to talk to you about the Brosno
Dragon . . .

STALIN: (excited) Ahh, da! If I had had an army of Brosnya Dragons, I would
have RULED THE WORLD!!! (coughs) I mean, the war, it would have been over . . .
much sooner . . . (choking up) . . . Oh, my Brosnya . . . my babushka . . . this
creature softened my heart of stone . . .

KLEERLEE: But Joe, how could you control such a monster?

STALIN: (snorts) Monster?! Monster??!! Fool! My Brosnya was like me! Scared
of no one! (screams) NO ONE!! She tore Nazi planes out of the sky! (maniacal
laughter) HAHAHAHAHAHAAAA! (Unintelligible whispering) Yes, Ivan Vasilyevich,
what is it . . . ?! (more unintelligible whispering) What's that?! The Glorious
Revolution has begun?! Excellent, Comrade! Excellent!

KLEERLEE: It sounds as though you're still busy, Joe, even in Hell . . .

STALIN: (chuckles) Hell, no! To me, this place is paradise! Now I must go, but
before I do, tovarishch, I will have you shot! Guards! Guards!! Guards!!! (Voice
trailing off)

RECORDING ENDS.

BROSNO DRAGON FACT FILE

Location: Lake Brosno, Tver region, Russia

Appearance: Dinosaur or dragon head, reptilian scales, long thin tail, sixteen feet long

Strength: You're joking, right? It catches airplanes in its teeth!

Weaknesses: Don't hold your breath!

Powers: It glows, man! It glows!

Fear Factor: 89.5

HOW TO CATCH THE BROSNO DRAGON

Play the national anthem of Russia,
better known as *Gosudarstvenny
Gimn Rossiyskoy Federatsii* (try
saying that with a mouthful of
jawbreakers!) at full blast. The
patriotic Brosnie will stand
to stiff attention throughout,
allowing you to throw a ginormous
net over it!

July — 29th

BUNYIP

Here's the most mix'n-match cryptid of them all!

In Australian Aboriginal folklore, the extremely aggressive and bloodthirsty Bunyip is described as having an emu's head and neck, a horse's mane and tail, and seal-like flippers, and is the size of a large bull.

Others claim it is a giant starfish, or a creature with a dog's head, walrus's tusks, sometimes with a horn, a duck's bill, seal's flippers, a horse's tail, and dark fur!

Or it has a seal's head, a fish's tail, and one large and one small flipper.

Other versions of the Bunyip include a horse's head, alligator's body and legs, stingray's tail, kangaroo's feet and tail, or giant chicken's legs. There are those who believe it to be an oversize bearded snake, a giant otter, a wombat, or even a frog.

The name Bunyip originates with the Wemba-Wemba (aka Wamba-Wamba) Aboriginal tribe in southwestern New South Wales, and means *devil* or *evil spirit*. It is sometimes referred to as *kianpratty*.

Paleontologists date the arrival of the Aboriginal tribes to Australia from Africa to around fifty thousand years ago, give or take a week.

It is possible that the Aboriginal culture is the world's oldest continuing culture, dating back at least seventy-five thousand years. (Although the San people of southern Africa may disagree! See the upcoming Dingonek chapter—we love a good argument!)

The Aboriginal people claim that they have lived in Australia since the time of Creation.

They came directly out of what they refer to as the Dreamtime of their creative ancestors. And the malevolent water spirit called Bunyip followed right behind them!

Hunting at night, the Bunyip happily devours any animal or person passing by its chosen water-hole lair.

Leaping out of hiding, it knocks its victim down before tearing out the human's throat with its deadly fangs, or eviscerating him with its piercing claws. Its favorite meal is the smooth flesh of young women and children.

Moments before attacking, it lets out an ear-rattling guttural screech, more powerful than a sonic boom. This isn't to allow prey the chance to escape but for enjoyment of the chase—the Bunyip likes to play with its food before eating it!

Case Study 913/56b

Fifteen-year-old Soul-Gon McDonald of Wollongong, New South Wales, Australia, has kindly allowed us to reproduce one of the entries in her monster-hunter diary.

G'day, Diary!

Well, cobber, this li'l goth girl only went 'n done it! I've been followin' th' blog o' that Yank ankle-biter Tobias Toombes 'n even if he does think he's th' ants' pants, he fair got me blood boilin' fer some serious monster-hunting action!

Fair dinkum, but I decided to avago! Y'know me, diary, I ain't no gunner—if I decide t'do summat, I do it!

So's I chucked a sickie from school, grabbed some tucker, 'n headed into th' Bush to a li'l billabong I know in th' Back o' Bourke to take a quick bo-peep for that grand pearler o' Aussie monsters—the Bunyip!

It was late arvo when I got there, and light was fallin' fast. Nothin' was stirrin' so I went walkabout to give th' place th' quick once-over.

Four hours later, 'n nothin'! I felt like a right drongo! I was about to head back when I heard it! This ear-poppin' screech 'n a rustlin' in th' bushes close by!

Next moment, th' li'l ripper only leaps straight out at me! Strewth, it was ugly as a box o' blowflies! It had this huge scaly head, dagger fangs; a furry body, striped tail 'n oversize chicken legs! Oh, yeah—'n freakin' wings!

Dinky-di, mate, I stood there like a stunned mullet! It was a li'l beauty! Then it leaned back on its haunches, ready to pounce! There was no escape!

That's when this young roo hopped by! Catchin' its movement, th' Bunyip changed course—and victim—'n attacked him! Th' li'l rug rat had no chance! I kicked up th' bull dust 'n I was outta there!

I'll never forget the poor joey's death screams, but sooner him than me!

My first monster hunt, diary, 'n it was grouse! Bonzer! Hooroo!

For those of you not well-versed in Aussie-speak, here are some translations:

G'day—hello

Cobber—friend

Ankle-biter—young child

Ants' pants—someone who has an unreasonably high opinion of themselves

Fair dinkum—absolutely true, genuine, honest

Avago—have a go (at doing something)

Gunner—indecisive ("He was gunner do this, gunner do that")

Summat—something

To chuck a sickie—to take an unofficial day off work or school

Tucker—food

Bush—the countryside, the Outback

Billabong—stagnant water caused by a blockage in a river

Back o' bourke—a long way away

Bo-peep—a sly look

Pearler—the very best, wonderful, excellent

Arvo—Afternoon

Walkabout—to wander around

Once-over—to look around

Drongo—a stupid person

Ripper—someone who is great, fantastic

Strewth—an exclamation of surprise

Box o' blowflies—really ugly

Dinky-di—the real thing, 100 percent true

A stunned mullet—extremely happy

Beaut, Beauty—Great, fantastic, wonderful

Roo/Joey—baby kangaroo

Rug rat—young kid

Bull dust—orange sand you find in the Outback

Grouse—tremendous

Bonzer—fantastic

Hooroo—good-bye

BUNYIP FACT FILE

Location: Rivers, billabongs, bogs, swamps and wells of Australia and Tasmania
Appearance: All kinds of everything!
Strength: You don't want to mess with it!
Weaknesses: Let's put it this way: No one has ever caught one—and lived!
Powers: With the various sightings of a Bunyip, there is a good chance it is a shape-shifter. It is also protected by "supernatural powers.
Fear Factor: 95.9

HOW TO ESCAPE A BUNYIP

Hold up a full-length mirror to the Bunyip. Even the Bunyip is confused as to what it looks like and will attack its reflection, thinking it is food! While it's tussling with itself, you can run for it!

.me 2. El Cuero

1a

1

2a

2

Drawn from Nature by Walter B. Lazarus

Stalking the rivers, lakes, and lagoons of the Patagonia region of South America, specifically in Argentina and much of Chile, is an aquatic monster like no other: *el Cuero!*

To the locals, *el Cuero* means "the Cowhide," although those of a Hispanic disposition will immediately cry foul, for *cuero* translated from Spanish literally means "skin" or "leather." The name actually refers to the creature's appearance, which looks like a cowhide that has been stretched out to dry.

This fiendish and extremely intelligent monstrosity is generally described as being between five and fifteen feet long, with wide pectoral fins lined with razor-sharp claws that are used to hold its prey.

Others claim that el Cuero has tentacles that end in razor-sharp forceps and two devil-red eyes! Whatever, it is one mugly dude! (For a more in-depth description, check out our ultra-awesome Case Study!)

A voracious predator, this charmer will eat almost anything, although it prefers prey that is easily overpowered, such as dogs, cats, and young children.

El Cuero waits patiently for a meal to pass by close to shore, then surges out of the water to attack its victim on land, its needle-sharp proboscis spearing through the skin to suck on blood and other bodily fluids and organs.

Naturally, it will also attack and kill anyone crazy enough to go drinking, swimming, fishing, or sailing near its home.

Another favorite el Cuero attack mode is to call upon the forces of dark magic! El Cuero uses demonic powers to levitate out of the water and hypnotize its prey. Unable to resist, they allow the beast to envelop and then crush or suffocate them in its huge fins before rolling them down to the lake bottom or riverbed to feast to its heart's delight.

Being quite a cleanliness fusspot, el Cuero later gathers up the bones and spits them back out onto dry land.

Case Study 27/Ec5

H.M.S. Beagle was an expedition and survey ship that set sail on its second voyage of discovery on December 27, 1831.

On board was a young naturalist named Charles Darwin. His findings during the five-year voyage helped Darwin to develop what came to be known as the Theory of Evolution or Natural Selection. Simply put, all life is related and has descended from a common ancestor.

On his return home on October 2, 1836, Darwin wrote a book about the voyage which he titled Journal and Remarks. This later became known as The Voyage of the Beagle.

We recently unearthed one of Darwin's "lost" journals. Inside, was an entry on a strange creature that Darwin discovered while exploring Patagonia. For some reason, he completely forgot to include this in his book. So for the first time ever, here is that entry!

(Plate 2. El Cuero)
Underside. 1a. Eye appendage. 2. Top. 2a. Fang.)

January 10, 1834

Leaving the *Beagle*, I took a boat to shore and made haste across Patagonia's wide and level desert plains. I was most anxious to investigate a large lake that I had set eyes upon as we arrived.

Reaching the water's edge, I noticed a collection of bones scattered close to shore. I immediately assumed these to be the remains of some animal that had been eaten by a much larger animal, thus enforcing my developing theory of natural selection——that only the fittest survive.

With growing apprehension, I quickly surmised my presumption to be false. These were not animal bones, but human, either from a dwarf adult or a child. What unspeakable horror could have perpetrated such an abominable act?!

A furious boiling and flailing of the water in the center of the lake caught my attention. From the hidden depths burst forth the foulest of creatures, a huge beast that resembled nothing less than a huge stingray.

I noticed that it appeared to have a cartilage skeleton. Its body was flattened, with serrated fins attached to the head and flowing down its sides.

On the end of each of its four red *ommatophores*——eyestalks——was the most hideous eye. Its underside revealed a gaping mouth with ghastly fangs and ventral gill slits, and a long, thin proboscis was clearly seen.

But the most amazing aspect of this beast was that it somehow *"levitated" in the air*! I stood transfixed, its eyes burning deep into my mind . . . my mind . . .

I awoke to find the creature gone. Terrified, I raced back to the ship to write down my encounter in this journal.

Everyone must know about this monster! I must not forget to tell the world . . . must . . . not . . . forget . . . must . . . not . . .

Here Darwin's entry mysteriously ends.

CHARLES DARWIN'S ENCOUNTER WITH EL CUERO JANUARY 10 1834.

EL CUERO FACT FILE

Location: The areas of Chile and Argentina in Patagonia, South America

Appearance: Stingray thingamajig, stalk-eyes, bloodsucking proboscis, fanged mouth

Strength: Demonic-fueled

Weaknesses: Leave branches from the calafate bush at the water's edge. El Cuero will wrap its body around the branches, thinking it to be prey. The bush's razor-sharp tripartite spines (spines split into three) will pierce its hide. Unable to pull free, el Cuero will slowly bleed to death! (Gross but effective!)

Powers: Dark magic, levitation, hypnotism

Fear Factor: 61

HOW TO CAPTURE EL CUERO

Erect a giant electrical fan beside the lake el Cuero is nesting in. On the opposite side of the lake, hang a large titanium steel net.

When el Cuero levitates out of the water to attack, switch on the fan and blow the sucker into the net! WHOOOSSSH!

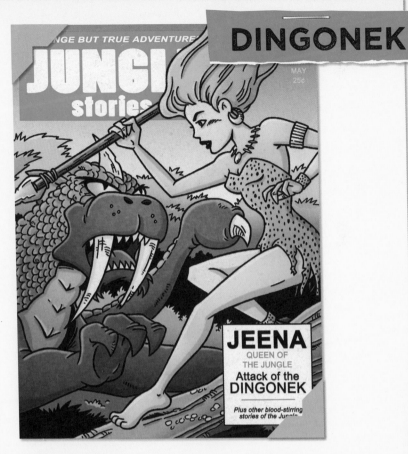

What do you get if you cross a giant scorpion with a saber-toothed walrus?

A creature you *seriously* wouldn't want to invite to your next pool party!

Dingonek has been freaking out honest folk in the African continent for millennia. Hanging out in the rivers and lakes of central and west Africa, most notably in the Democratic Republic of the Congo and Kenya, this truly horrifying cryptid is described as between twelve and eighteen feet long.

Its square head and long horn with thick armadillo scales fashionably complements its saber teeth, reptilian claws, and extended bony tail that ends in a deadly scorpion's dart, the sting from which means instant death!

Dingonek has been sighted on numerous occasions by the indigenous San people of southern Africa. Arguably one of the world's most ancient races, these hunter-gatherers are spread out cross the Kalahari Desert in search of food.

Camping in temporary shelters, rocky overhangs, and caves, the proud San people are considered to be the descendants of early Stone Age humans, and have lived in southern Africa for over seventy thousand years.

Their knowledge and wisdom is unsurpassed, and if they claim that Dingonek exists, then we believe them!

Proof of this came in an extraordinary archaeological discovery in the caves of Brakfontein Ridge in South Africa.

San rock art is considered to be some of the best artistic representations of animals and humans of its kind. On one of the walls, a painting dating back tens of thousands of years depicts an unknown animal that is the exact replica of the Dingonek, right down to its tusks!

Extremely territorial, Dingonek nests in shallow waters, feasting on crocodiles, hippos, and any foolhardy fishermen who think they can disturb the Dingonek's peace and not pay the ultimate price!

John Alfred Jordan (b. circa 1856) was an English traveler, big-game hunter, and trader (i.e., he killed beautiful animals for fun and profit. Way to go, John! Your mom would be so proud!), and the African continent's most notorious ivory poacher. He once slaughtered thirty-eight crocodiles in one day on Lake Victoria.

In 1907, on the banks of the River Maggori in Kenya, Jordan took a shot at Dingonek—but the bullet merely bounced off its thick hide!

"Gad, but he was a hideous old haunter of a nightmare, was that beast-fish," Jordan later revealed in an interview. "Blast that blighter's fangs, but they looked long enough to go clean through a man. I gave him a .303 hard-nose behind his leopard ear, and then hell split for fair." (And yes, fancy English people really did used to speak in that ridiculous affected manner—and some still do, even today! By Jove! The bounders!)

Case Study 273/55d

Pulp magazines were popular and inexpensive fiction magazines published from 1896 until the mid 1950s. The name comes from the cheap wood-pulp paper they were printed on.

Their stories were mostly lurid and sensational. The best-selling Jungle Stories featured exciting tales based on true events. We are proud to reprint a story extract featuring their most popular character: Jeena, Queen of the Jungle!

Attack of the Dingonek!

Chapter XII

The eviscerated body of Kwame pumped its remaining lifeblood into the arid dust, turning the ground a dark shade of death. He had been Jeena's teacher, her friend! Now his spirit had joined those of his ancestors in the afterworld.

The Jungle Queen choked back hot, stinging tears. "Forgive me, Kwame!" she cried out, her grief raw and embittered. "I should have been here to protect you!"

Her emerald cat's eyes glistening brightly in the afternoon sunlight, a snake's sibilant hiss escaping her berry-red lips, she swore, softly, "Dingonek, beware!

Vengeance . . . is mine! Oooooleeee-aaaa-leeee-ooooooloooooo!"

Jeena's savage battle cry echoed across the thick jungle expanse. Silence descended. When Jeena spoke, the jungle listened!

Lowering her eyes, Jeena swayed gently, allowing herself to connect to the animal kingdom she ruled over.

Channeling the magnified hearing of the barn owl, Jeena quickly detected the heavy footfalls of the death-dealing Dingonek, some distance away!

Her eyes snapped open! Snatching up her prized spear, the magnificent Jungle Queen called upon the agile ability of the spider monkey!

Leaping high to catch the branch of a baobab tree, she began swinging from tree to tree with cheetah swiftness.

One thousand jungle drumbeats later, Jeena dropped from on high to land at the banks of a fast-flowing river. Before her was a terrifying sight——A monstrous beast that defied sane description!

Three times Jeena's height, with a body of golden scales, an elongated horn piercing through its forehead, razor-sharp claws, and a distended tail that ended with a grotesque and venomous stinger!

DINGONEK!

A nightmarish demon born in hell's nursery and released upon an unsuspecting world, Dingonek called no one master but Satan himself!

With an ear-bursting roar, Dingonek charged to attack! *RRROOAARRR!*

The bloody battle to the death had begun! And there could be only one survivor!

DINGONEK FACT FILE

Location: African continent, notably central, western, and southern Africa
Appearance: Trust us; you'll know it when you see it!
Strength: Yipes!
Weaknesses: You ask—we're too scared!
Powers: Bulletproof, superpowered leaps, speed-swimming, scorpion's death-sting
Fear Factor: Off the charts

WHAT TO DO WITH A DINGONEK

Train it as a guard dog, and the next time you ditch school for the day, your folks won't be receiving a visit from the truancy officer! (Not that we're encouraging such practices, you understand!) (*Ahem!*)

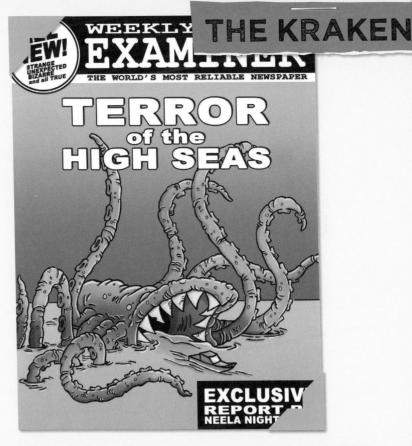

Oceanic monstrosities come in all shapes and sizes, but the mightiest colossus **OF!!! THEM!!! ALL!!!** is the senses-shattering leviathan only spoken about in dread whispers by sailors—the Kraken!

For those who think Aspidochelone is "rather big," he is but a dust mote compared to this dude! The body circumference of an adult male Kraken can reach 1.5 *miles*, with a tentacle length of over nine hundred feet! And each of its eight tentacles may have up to one thousand suckers on it!

This tentacled monstrosity lives in the deepest depths of the oceans, far deeper than humans have ever reached!

Like other aquatic and land animals, the Kraken possesses the ability to camouflage

91

itself, adapting its color to suit its surroundings, changing from bright greens and reds to a sandy orange. (This is a chemical process known as *metachrosis*.)

Existing before the first dinosaurs walked the Earth 230 million years ago, the Kraken survived the cataclysmic event that wiped them out 164 million years later.

The first written account of the beast appears in the Old Norwegian scientific work *Konungs skuggsjá* ("King's mirror"), published circa 1250 by an anonymous author who encountered the creature as he crossed the Greenland Sea

In the latter part of the twelfth century, the sea monster is again referred to in the Old Icelandic saga *Örvar-Odds saga* ("The Saga of Örvar-Odds," The story of a legendary Icelandic hero who name means "Arrow-Point" or "Arrow-Odd"): "It is its nature that it swallows both men and ships and whales and everything that it can reach."

The story reveals that the Kraken belches a good one, hacking up digested food and vomiting it onto the ocean surface to attract more food: "It is said to be the nature of these fish that when one shall desire to eat, then it stretches up its neck with a great belching, and following this belching comes forth much food."

Vast schools of fish come to dine on the Kraken's Technicolor chunder (vomit) and are then themselves swallowed up in its mouth, which the author claims is as big as a fjord! (FYI: One of the fjords in Scoresby Sund in Greenland is the world's longest at 217.5 miles.)

In the first edition of his book *Systema Naturae*, published in 1735, in which he classified living organisms by their shared characteristics (a process known as *taxonomy*), famed Swedish physician, botanist, and zoologist Carl Linnaeus (1707–1778) classified the Kraken as a *cephalopod* (a marine animal with a prominent head and tentacles). He gave the creature the cool-sounding scientific name *Microcosmus marinus*.

Even English poet Alfred, Lord Tennyson (1809–1892), cashed in on the Kraken's celeb status when he wrote an irregular fifteen-line sonnet he called *The Kraken* in 1830. Here's a taste:

> Below the thunders of the upper deep;
> Far, far beneath in the abysmal sea,
> His ancient, dreamless, uninvaded sleep
> The Kraken sleepeth.

Case Study 936/5tk

Neela Nightshade, ace reporter for the Weekly World
Examiner, recently filed this report.

TERROR OF THE HIGH SEAS

Weekly World Examiner Exclusive

Greenland Sea, October 13

Day six, and the thick ice-laden fog, chill wind, and choppy seas make heavy
going for the two research vessels hired by this newspaper to hunt down the
Kraken. With temperatures rarely rising above freezing, spirits on board are,
like our bodies, lethargic. But the Kraken *is* out there! I can sense it!

My vessel has a stockpile of depth charges, a close-in weapon system (CIWS),
and multiple-barrel rapid-fire medium-caliber guns. Our companion ship is
likewise protected. If the Kraken comes looking for a fight, we'll give him one!

At least, that was the plan! It all starts to go horribly wrong three hours
later. A shout from the captain! A huge shape has been detected moving upward
from the depths at unimaginable speeds!

Before anyone can react, the roiling waters burst asunder all around us!

A hideous, soul-scarring screech fills our ears, transfixing us in abject
terror! In cinematic slo-mo, the Kraken rises forth from beneath the waves,
reaching a height that dwarfs the tallest skyscraper!

With screams and shouts echoing all around me, I inwardly smile. The
creature is magnificent! There is a beauty in its terrible ugliness, its
flailing giant tentacles sinuously dancing a glorious *adagio* in front of me!

Then—the rapid death-chatter of guns and miniature missile explosions
against the beast's impenetrable hide!

With an angry shriek, the monster whips out a many-suckered tentacle,
seizing our companion vessel and lifting it high above his head!

The ship snaps in two, men falling to their deaths in the churning waters or else into the Kraken's gaping maw! Their death cries will live with me forever!

The Kraken quickly dives back down to the ocean depths, and in doing so creates a treacherous whirlpool that threatens to sink our ship!

We survive—just barely! And I come away from this terrifying ordeal with photographic proof that the Gargantua of the Seas really does exist!

THE KRAKEN FACT FILE

Location: Atlantic and Arctic oceans; Norwegian, Greenland, and Mediterranean seas

Appearance: Monstrous squid-type with eight giant tentacles

Strength: Our advice? Don't challenge it to an arm-wrestling contest!

Weaknesses: You're kidding, right?!

Powers: Creates giant whirlpools, camouflage expert (can disguise itself as an island), belching champion

Fear Factor: 99.1

HOW TO CAPTURE THE KRAKEN

Tell it jokes! No, really! The Kraken has a great sense of humor! Once it starts laughing, it can't stop!

And while it's suffering from a giggle fit, you can grab it, bag it, tag it, and sell to an aquarium! (Hey, let them figure out how to build a tank big enough to hold it!)

LLAMHIGYN Y DWR

Stock up on your daffodils and leeks because we're heading for that most mystical and magical of all the countries that make up the United Kingdom . . . *Cymru*!

What do you mean you've never heard of it? We're not surprised! It's the locals' Celtic name for *Wales*! (FYI: *Cymru* is actually pronounced *kem-ri*.)

Llamhign y Dwr (pronounced—in a really cool Welsh accent—*Thlam-hee-gin er door*) has been around long before *Homo sapiens* first set foot in Wales some twenty-nine thousand years ago. (And seventeen to nineteen thousand years later, Mesolithic hunter-gathers from central Europe popped over for a weekend break and decided to make the mountainous landscape their permanent crib.)

Residing in swamps and marshes, rivers, streams, lakes, and ponds, Llamhign y Dwr, a fanged carnivorous *anghenfil*—Welsh for *monster*—may look cute with its limbless froggy/toady body, bat's wings, and lizard's tail, but try cuddling this beast and it will rip your heart out, quite literally!

Otherwise known as the Water Leaper for its ability to leap out of the water and glide through the air, Llamhigyn y Dwr can reach enormous size. Both fishermen and shepherds live in mortal terror of the beast!

It bursts forth from the water, screeching hideously. Sinking its fangs into its victim's neck, this amphibious abomination rips out his throat or else snaps the fishing line and pulls its terrified prey into the water to devour him!

Case Study 822/8lyd

The Mabinogion (pronounced Mabin-o-Gion) is a book collecting eleven exciting fantasy stories that first appeared in either one or both of the medieval Welsh manuscripts *Llyfr Gwyn Rhydderch* (White Book of Rhydderch) written around 1350, and *Llyfr Coch Hergest* (Red Book of Hergest) written between 1382 and 1410. The stories themselves were written much earlier, dating back to at least the eleventh and twelfth century.

These epic tales include five Welsh versions of adventures featuring King Arthur and the Knights of the Round Table.

Well, Welsh historians *thought* there were only eleven stories, but you know us! We've unearthed a twelfth story that was somehow left out of *The Mabinogion*!

Celyn

He was Celyn, son of Caw and one of the messengers between Arthur and his cousin Culhwch at the bloody Battle of Camlann in the year 537. The final battle for the great king who was most mortally wounded by his viper enemy Mordred.

At this time, Celyn was a high-spirited young man, in the prime of life and flower of youth, eager to prove his bravery at every opportunity.

With the death of the emperor Arthur, Celyn's warrior's fighting spirit momentarily deserted him, a heavy weariness descended upon his heart, and he sought solace awhile in his own company.

For ninety days and ten he did ride alone across the length and breadth of Cymru, until such time as he came upon a large lake in a forest of Cardigan. His horse, in much need of rest, indicated its wish to stop there to drink.

Dismounting, Celyn led the horse to the water's edge and then lay down to doze in the warm sunshine, fleetingly wondering whether he would ever regain his brash eagerness to fight another battle.

His dark thoughts were interrupted by a huge, dreadful commotion: a violent thrashing and flailing of the water and the terrified braying of his horse!

Leaping up out of the lake and screeching most frightfully was a monstrous form the likes of which Celyn's eyes had never beheld!

A good half size again to his horse, the grotesque beast had the bloated body of a toad, giant bat wings, and a thrashing lizard's tail with venomous stinger!

"Ho, there, Satan's pet!" the young soldier cried, unsheathing his sword. "Stay thy fangs or feel the bite of my blade!"

The monster let out an almighty squeal and plunged toward him at unimaginable speed!

No time had he but to raise his weapon before the creature struck! Its powerful form knocked Celyn off his feet, the heavy impact forcing the sword from his hand!

This supernatural horror was immediately upon him, shrieking so loudly his ears did bleed, its leathered wings battering him senseless! Would he soon be joining his most noble king in the spirit world, he wondered?

Through the creature's pummeling appendages, Celyn then did see a sight to gladden his heart. Surging up from the lake was a majestic figure Celyn knew well.

Bathed in heaven's golden light, it was a man of towering height and presence, wrapped in a powerful frame of muscle and sinew. His grizzled features partially hidden by a thick red beard, he wore the very chain mail and crown he wore in final battle.

Arthur Pendragon, Defender of all Britain!

Celyn's spirits soaring, he threw off his attacker and leaped for his sword. The winged terror flew in close, attempting to whip him with its venomous tail.

The young man twisted sharply, bringing up his sword to cleave the beast clean in two! It fell dead at his feet!

Panting heavily, Celyn looked over to the lake, but Arthur was there no longer. It mattered not.

Celyn had found his warrior's heart once more.

LLAMHIGYN Y DWR FACT FILE

Location: Wales
Appearance: Frog/toad-bat-lizard hybrid
Strength: Strong
Weaknesses: Most weapons will kill Llamhigyn y Dwr—if it gives you the chance, that is!
Powers: Flight, speed-swimming, venomous tail
Fear Factor: 49

HOW TO DEFEAT LLAMHIGYN Y DWR

Sneak up on Llamy while he's resting out of the water and—mondo yucky, we know—*kiss him* on the lips!

If he turns into a handsome prince, you'll totally own him for life! If he doesn't . . . well, you won't be around to worry about it!

In our humble opinion, this is one of the most sick-nasty aqua monsters around! Why? 'Cause if it catches you, it will devour your face, crack open your skull, and suck out your brains! Slamming!

The Xhosa and Zulu tribes of South Africa have tagged this demonic entity the Brain Sucker, and they should know, since a high number of deaths are suspected of being the result of Mamlambo's gruesome MO (*modus operandi*—Latin for "method of operation").

Living beneath the waters of the Mzintlava River, close to Mount Ayliff, a small town in the Eastern Cape province, Mamlambo can reach an astonishing length of sixty-seven feet with the head of a horse, the body of a fish (sometimes with crocodile scales), short stumpy legs, and a serpent's neck.

But the biggest kicker is that to the Zulu people Mamlambo is a *goddess*, the name translating to "goddess of rivers," who controls all the rivers flowing through the province of KwaZulu Natal, an area roughly the size of Indiana.

Travel note: The Zulu people are the largest ethnic group in South Africa, with approximately ten to eleven million people, mostly living in KwaZulu Natal, although small numbers can also be found in Mozambique, Zambia, Tanzania, and Zimbabwe. The word *Zulu* (aka iZulu, iliZulu, or liTulu) means *heaven* or *sky*.

The Xhosa people believe Mamlambo to be a giant river snake who will grant wealth and good fortune to anyone who captures it in exchange for setting it free again.

Appearing during violent thunderstorms, Mamlambo, like the Brosno Dragon, is bioluminescent, glowing ghostly green in the dark!

In common with el Cuero, it has two large green eyes that it uses to hypnotize its prey, luring them to the water's edge before dragging them down to the murky depths, there to feast on their brain matter and suck their corpse dry of blood! Some cryptologists argue that Mamlambo may be the only surviving specimen of the mosasaur, a carnivorous marine reptile from the late Cretaceous period (100.5 to 66 million years ago), which could reach lengths of fifty-seven feet and was the top aquatic predator, totally owning the world's seas.

Case Study 133/50m

The following report was obtained under the Freedom of Information Act. It was filed by an agent of the Central Bureau of Investigation, the clandestine American government agency that investigates all paranormal sightings. Dates, names, and specific locations have been redacted to protect the innocent.

Rock Hardy

C.B.I. Special Agent

Case No: 772/00M ------------

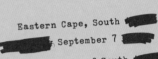

Eastern Cape, South ▓▓▓▓
▓▓▓▓, September 7 ▓▓▓▓

Located at the southern tip of Africa, the Republic of South ▓▓▓▓ is home to almost 49 million people. Its 1,739 miles of coastline is divided into nine provinces.

This agent came at the behest of the Eastern Cape province authorities who were concerned that some type of aquatic monster called Mamlambo is feeding on their populace and scaring away potential tourists.

It all sounded like a fisherman's tall tale if you ask this agent, but then this agent is not paid to think——he's paid to act.

And act this agent did, setting up a Base of Operations Command Post close to the shore of the ▓▓▓▓ River, where the beast supposedly encamped.

While awaiting the "monster's" appearance, this agent interviewed locals who claimed to have seen Mamlambo in action. The Xhosa speak the Bantu language and are part of the Nguni people, who migrated from the Great Lakes areas of Africa more than two thousand years ago.

"It eats their faces off and sucks out the people's brains," said elderly Mr. ▓▓▓▓, walking the lonely track with his dogs. "It is a big snake, and I have seen what it does."

Eight days and nights this agent scouted the area around the swirling river. As he suspected——nothing! He was about to request a transfer back to headquarters when a violent thunderstorm struck the province. The rain fell in a thick curtain, swelling the river in mere moments!

Through howling winds, this agent's keen hearing picked up a loud high-pitched wailing. Straining to see clearly though the heavy downpour, he made out a shape rising up from the river. As jagged lightning ripped asunder the darkened sky, this agent believed he saw a giant horse towering above him, two saucer-size eyes blazing a luminescent green!

The horse's neck seemed to elongate until its head towered above this agent. It reached down and grabbed this agent's head in its mouth before lifting him up and tossing him carelessly aside like a rag doll! This agent smashed to the ground, his breath forcefully expelled from his body! As quickly as it developed, the thunderstorm disappeared. The river was calm once more.

This agent believes that the raging atmospherics caused him to suffer temporary insanity. He was no doubt picked up by the swirling winds, which did possess the strength of a powerful whirlwind.

Regarding the Mamlambo, this agent found no evidence of its existence. As per agreement with Regional Supervisor ████████, this agent respectfully suggests that this case be closed, and not be presented to the relevant authorities on paranormal activities.

MAMLAMBO FACT FILE

Location: Eastern Cape, South Africa
Appearance: Horse/fish/croc/serpent conglomeration
Strength: Mighty tough!
Weaknesses: The Xhosa people claim Mamlambo can be caught . . . but they refuse to tell us quite how to do it! Thanks, guys! Appreciate it!
Powers: Hypnotism, glow-in-the-dark righteousness!
Fear Factor: 71.4

HOW TO KILL MAMLAMBO

Place a remote-controlled bomb in the head of a dummy and float it across the river. When Mamlambo pulls it down to the riverbed to feast on its brain—*KAAAA-BOOOOOM!*

From the most monstrous aqua beast to the world's most famous and well-loved—Nessie!

Nessie—called the Loch Ness Monster by reason of the fact that she dwells in a *loch* (the Scottish Gaelic word for lake) in the Scottish Highlands close to the small picturesque village of Drumnadrochit (population roughly 813)—has been playing hide-and-seek with humans for at least fifteen hundred years, and probably much longer that that!

Although Loch Ness is ten thousand years old, Nessie's first official sighting came on August 22 in the year 565 when one of the Church's loyal servants, the Irish missionary monk Saint Columba (AD 521–597) decided he needed a break from converting all the "heathens" to Christianity and took a vacation to Scotland.

Coming across local men burying a companion besides the River Ness (the river that leads off from the Loch), Saint Columba was informed that the man had been mauled to death by a giant savage creature hiding in the water.

Being the really brave dude that he was, Saint Columba ordered his *servant* to go for a swim in the river, and lo and behold, up popped Nessie to snack on another human. Luckily, St. Columba said a quick prayer and Nessie halted as if "pulled back by ropes." Terrified by this divine intervention, she fled in terror and the relieved servant gratefully thanked the Lord for the miracle.

Nessie wasn't seen again, at least not officially, until 1933, when she was seen four times in as many months. One of the sightings was reported to a journalist working for the *Inverness Courier*. The Scottish newspaper published the story in their May 2, 1933, edition, and suddenly Nessie became a worldwide celeb!

Since then, she has been seen more than three thousand times, with at least twenty-five sightings reported each year!

All reports tell of a cryptid thirty to fifty feet in length, having a small head, a gaping red mouth, long snake-like neck, two large humps, and a tail.

Nicknamed Nessie by locals (*Niseag* in Scottish Gaelic), she is usually seen gliding under the surface of the loch before diving back down to the depths.

And Loch Ness is seriously deep! And big! There is more water in this loch than in all the lakes in England and Wales put together! It is 755 feet at its deepest spot; it is 22.6 miles long, and is 1.7 miles at its widest.

The loch contains a mind-boggling 263 billion cubic feet of water and has a surface area of 13,952 acres/21.8 square miles. It could hold the world's entire population of seven billion humans *ten times over*!

Nessie is a great monster for newbie hunters to try catching. Aside from the poor soul back in AD 565, she has never, so far as we know, killed another human. Go, Nessie!

Case Study 044/91n

English fisherman Rod N. Line went on a fishing trip to Loch Ness. He later wrote an article for the popular American fishing magazine *Big Catch*. We reproduce his article below.

The One That Got Away,

Loch Ness in the fall is the perfect place for the dedicated angler. The rowdy tourists hoping to spot sight of a nonexistent aquatic dinosaur have by now mostly departed.

The brittle sharpness of approaching winter hangs on the gently stirring breeze, and the leaves begin turning a rustic orange and brown as if to camouflage the surrounding landscape from passersby.

An eeriness settles over the loch. Steering my rented boat across the dark waters, the dank color created by floating peat particles, I stare out across the vast panorama and realize that I am all alone.

Brown trout being my catch of the day, I set up three rods, each one a spin-casting heavy-action rig six to seven feet, the line spool enclosed in housing mounted near the top of the rod.

Trout are found between thirty and a hundred feet below the surface of the loch, and I am using my favorite choice for natural bait, aquatic larvae known as *hellgrammites*, alongside the usual grasshoppers, earthworms, and leeches.

Seven hours I sat in the middle of Ness with no luck, and I was about to call it a day when one of the rods jerked violently. A catch!

Leaping to action, I began to reel in, realizing too late that this was much more than a mere trout. I was almost pulled from the boat by the massive weight, and the extreme effort threatened to snap my rod in two.

Glancing down, my eyes sighted a large shape rocketing toward the surface. A giant eel? Surely not! Abruptly, the water exploded upward, and there before me was the creature I publicly mocked—the heart-stopping terror known as the Loch Ness Monster!

Her booming roar reverberated across the loch, my hook still caught in her upper lip! The thrashing serpentine neck rising high, she dove toward the boat!

Screaming in mortal fear, I leaped overboard seconds before Nessie caught the boat in her mouth and disappeared with it back under the murky depths!

Without waiting for a return match, I swam desperately to shore. The biggest catch I ever had, and the one that got away!

NESSIE FACT FILE

Location: Loch Ness, Scotland, UK
Appearance: It's Nessie!! ('Nuff said!)
Strength: The strength to pull in two million tourists every year to see a big lake
Weaknesses: Can't resist showing off for the tourists
Powers: Scotland's most profitable tourist attraction and souvenir seller
Fear Factor: 5
Endearment Factor: 1,000,000,000,000

HOW TO CAPTURE NESSIE
(At least on film!)

leo 1477

Considered all that and a bag of chips by many monster hunters, the Sirens are beautiful half-woman/half-bird hybrids.

They are closely related to mermaids, the half-woman/half-fish creatures who first appeared in the waters around the kingdom of Assyria in 1000 BC. (Assyria existed from around 2500 BC until 609 BC, close to the Upper Tigris River in Mesopotamia—present-day northern Iraq, including parts of Syria, Turkey, and a smidgen of Iran.)

Like their mermaid cousins, the Sirens (*Seirenes* in Greek) are vicious, murdering sea nymphs (naiads) who delight in mesmerizing sailors with their enchanted singing. Entranced, the sailors smash their ships onto jagged rocks and drown.

The Sirens were originally found on Sirenum Scopuli, three small rocky islands between

Sorrento and Capri in the Mediterranean, and later spread farther around, turning up in the waters of northern and eastern Europe, the Middle East, and Asia.

Although there are at least five known Sirens luring feebleminded men to their watery graves, the three most famous of these femmes fatales are the sisters Peisinoe, Aglaope, and Thelxiepeia, either the daughters of the Greek river god Achelous or the sea god Phorcys.

Their appearance (depending upon how much strong grog a sailor has drunk) is a creature with either a woman's or bird's head, a woman's or bird's body, with or without wings, and a woman's/bird's/scaly fish's feet or a fish's tail.

The Sirens' first starring role was in the *Odyssey*, an epic poem written by the blind Greek poet Homer in the late eighth century BC. (And when we say epic, we mean epic! *The Odyssey* runs to 12,110 lines! Yipes!)

Pliny the Elder, writing in Book Ten of his thirty-seven–book magnum opus (his greatest work) *Naturalis Historia*, dismissed the Sirens as pure fable, although he admitted that the celebrated Greek historian and writer Dinon attested that "they exist in India, and that they charm men by their song, and, having first lulled them to sleep, tear them to pieces."

Jump almost fifteen hundred years to *da Man* Leonardo da Vinci (1452–1519), the great Italian Renaissance painter, sculptor, musician, inventor, architect, mathematician, engineer, cartographer, geologist, botanist, writer . . . well, the dude was a freaking genius at a lot of things! Check him out!

Anyhow, in his notebooks he writes, "The Siren sings so sweetly that she lulls the mariners to sleep; then she climbs upon the ships and kills the sleeping mariners."

Case Study 946/20s

Captain James Cook (1728–1779) was a famed English explorer, navigator, and cartographer. He was the first European to explore eastern Australia, which he named New South Wales, and the first to visit Hawaii.

His first voyage (1768-1771) to the South Pacific Ocean to observe the transit of Venus across the sun saw young Lieutenant James Cook take command of the H.M.S. Endeavour.

Cook kept a detailed ship's log of the voyage. When the log was eventually published, one passage was mysteriously removed on orders of King George III himself. Until now, that is!

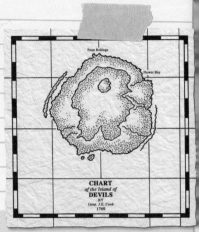

CHART
of the Island of
DEVILS
BY
Lieut. J.E. Cook
1769

A JOURNAL OF THE PROCEEDINGS OF HIS MAJESTY'S BARK *ENDEAVOUR* ON A VOYAGE AROUND THE WORLD BY LIEUTENANT JAMES COOK

Commander, Commencing the 25th of May, 1768.

(April 1769, on course for Tahiti)

Wednesday 5th. A fresh, steady breeze and fine weather. At I p.m. made Sail to the Westward, and at 1/2 past 3 saw land to the North-West, which proved to be a low woody Island of a Circular form, and not much above a Mile in Compass.

Of a sudden a strange Affliction came upon both Seamen and Gentlemen.
(Note: Gentlemen is Cook's name for the civilians aboard ship.)

A haunting melody was heard drifting on the gentle breeze, one that momentarily entranced all on board.

Myself feeling most Light-headed, I left Cabin and made for Deck to find Seamen and Gentlemen standing group'd together at Starboard, staring glaz'd-eyed toward the Island.

Three beautiful Women sat in a Flowery Meadow, one playing the Lute, one a Harp, and a third she was Singing. I Deduc'd immediately that these were no ordinary Women, for they had bird-like feather'd Bodies, large Wings, and Scaly Feet.

The Sounds were at once both entrancing and nauseating. My mind did swirl and I threaten'd to lose all Consciousness.

To my Horror, I helplessly did watch one of the Seamen of but 14 Years in Age, Ship's Boy Albert Rollings, step forth from the Deck and drop into the calm Sea. He did not resurface. A second Seaman follow'd his strange Actions, and then a Third.

Realizing at once that these Women were the deadly Sirens of Legend, I took up a handful of Tar from the Barrel and made haste to fill the Ears of everyone on Board, myself included.

Momentarily Deaf to All Sound, I signall'd the Seamen to make Haste and Set Sail away from this Devil's Island and by God's Holy Grace we thus did Survive our terrible Encounter.

THE SIRENS FACT FILE

Location: Most anywhere there's the sea, rocks, and good acoustics!
Appearance: Beautiful woman, feathery bird, scaly fish
Strength: They can bump off shiploads of men with a mere song!
Weaknesses: Pull out their feathers and they die . . . but getting close enough is the tricky part!
Powers: Hypnotic singing voice, cool harp- and lyre-playing
Fear Factor: 52.1

WHAT TO DO WITH CAPTURED SIRENS

Enter them into a TV talent contest. Their hypnotic voices guarantee they'll win. Then fame, fortune, and mega-celeb status will be theirs—and as their promoter/manager, yours, too! Woo-hoo!

TARASQUE

This sickly dank water beastie has an on fire pedigree, being the offspring of the Bonnacon (aka **Bonocon** and **Bonasus**, a dragon-like creature from Asia) and the Leviathan, the demon sea monster mentioned in the Bible, who demonologists say is one of the seven princes of hell!

Tarasque (pronounced *tar-rask*) has a lion's head and a curved spike-covered turtle shell over an ox or bison-like body. The rest of its frame has overlapping scales, making it armor-plated!

Complementing this are six short bear-like legs with slice-'n-dice razor-sharp claws, in addition to a long, scaly tail that ends in a huge scorpion's sting.

Its teeth are "as sharp as swords" and it can breathe fire "the space of an acre of land"! (An acre is 76 percent the size of a football field.)

With "the strength of twelve lions," Tarasque has been savaging people at least as far back as 200 BC, and no doubt many millennia before this.

In the nineteenth century, archaeologists unearthed a stone statue of Tarasque in a French cemetery and dated its origin to the La Tène cultural and artistic movement. (La Tène developed in eastern France, Switzerland, Austria, southwest Germany, and some Slav countries, notably the Czech Republic, Poland, Slovakia, Slovenia, Hungary, and Romania, during the Late Iron Age from 450 BC until the first century AD.)

During the first century, Tarasque went on a violent killing spree in the town of Nerluc, close to the Rhône River in France. No one could stop its bloody rampage!

Martha of Bethany arrived in the town and wasted no time in facing down the monster.

Quenching its fire with holy water, she handed Tarasque over to the townspeople, who set about stoning to death the now-defenseless animal.

Overcome by their own wickedness, they converted to Martha's new religion of Christianity and built a church in her name. They renamed the town Tarascon.

However . . . no one in the town noticed that the body of the Tarasque had mysteriously *disappeared*! It popped up again in the town in 1448, and was supposedly killed by Jean d'Arlatan, attendant to King René (1409–1480). Nevertheless, once again, the Tarasque's body vanished!

Throughout its missing millennia and up to the present day, Tarasque has been regularly seen swimming the waters of Hạ Long Bay in Vietnam, chomping down on helpless fishermen. (Hạ Long Bay is named *Vinh Hạ Long* in Vietnamese, literally "descending dragon bay," and is a UNESCO World Heritage Site.)

Case Study 4545/45t

King Henry VIII (1491–1547) took the throne of England when he was a mere sapling of nineteen. He became one of the cruelest and most tyrannical of all English kings. During his reign over seventy-two thousand people were executed, averaging out at between four and five people per day, every day, for thirty-eight years!

In 1535, Henry got into a disagreement with the Church, and during the next six years closed down most of the monasteries in England, Wales, and Ireland. Those friars and monks who survived Henry's violent purge found themselves on the unemployment line.

One such was the Franciscan friar Brother Jacob, who decided to go into the monster-hunting business. He kept a record of his encounters with Satan's demonic hordes, and we have great pleasure in reprinting an excerpt of one of these tales below.

The Adventures of Brother Jacob

"Dost thou knowest the time?" I asked Beelzebub's most pestilent of foul creatures, "It is time for a Reckoning. Thou must pay for thy vast catalogue of sins, but before that die is cast, repent, and the Lord shall have mercy upon thy blackened soul!"

Glancing past the great behemoth before me, I sighed wearily at the sight of an entire French village burned to hot ash and cinders, its inhabitants no more. The devilish work of Tarasque!

This hideous nightmare made real let out a ground-trembling roar of displeasure amid a fiery blast of hellspawned flame. Only

my acrobat's skills allowed me to back-flip over the attack, although my beard was still sorely singed!

"Fie, sirrah, thou art a villain of the grandest magnitude," I cried, hurriedly patting out my smoking facial hairs. "These were God's holy hairs that you have defamed. For this, thou shalt pay the ultimate price!"

With that, I swung my mighty battle-ax against the monster's scaly hide . . . and watched in horror as the metal blade shattered into pieces!

How could it be thus? The foul fiend was defying God's divine warrior!

Then, when all seemed but lost, I fleetingly recalled the beatific Saint Martha's teachings whence she too had battled yon foe.

Pulling forth my small vial of Holy Water and with a quick prayer and the Lord's guiding hand, I threw it into Tarasque's opened mouth!

A scream most detestable echoed from the abomination and it staggered, its eyes weeping blood!

"Thou art dead; no physician's art can save thee!" I cried triumphantly, momentarily breaking one of the sacred Ten Commandments. I knew God would forgive me.

As to the beast, it ran pell-mell into the deep river adjacent to the village, disappearing from sight, ne'er to return!

Hallelujah!

TARASQUE FACT FILE

Location: France, Vietnam
Appearance: Gruesome!
Strength: Herculean!
Weaknesses: None!
Powers: Hypnotic stare! Fire-breathing! Revolting bad breath! Undeadable!
Fear Factor: Oodles! (98.8!)

What to Do with a Captured Tarasque

Use its hot breath to power the heating system in your chilly castle!

SEA OF JAPAN SAFETY

Yamamoto Daichi

Guide to
Dangerous Marine Animals

LLB
Publishing

Staying with our religious theme, we arrive at the scary Japanese Umibōzu (aka *Umi boshi* and *umi nyudo*). This literally translates as "sea monk." Its name derives from its resemblance to the large round head of a Buddhist monk.

Its length may be as short as a few feet, or it may be the size of a mountain!

A well-known shape-shifter, Umibōzu may look like a giant cloud or shadow, opaque gray or black, with no hair or eyes, or else with oily skin and large glowing eyes.

It may have small arms held close to its chest and giant elongated tentacles, or else arms and legs that look like snakes!

Umibōzu has also been seen as a hairy beast the size of a whale, or a beautiful woman who lures sailors into her arms before turning into a hideous, screeching monster!

Then again, it may be light brown with orange eyes, a croc's mouth, the tail of a shrimp, and the moo of a cow! (Really!)

Or perhaps it may be dark brown with no nose or mouth, eyes six inches in diameter, and deeply wrinkled skin!

More commonly, it appears as a giant black hairless head with huge eyes!

Heck, who knows? But fearful sailors understand that every time they set sail, Umibōzu may be waiting to greet them!

Our advice? Don't panic! Umibōzu isn't the sharpest pencil in the box, and there are ways to defeat it.

The little versions of Umibōzu don't take kindly to being whacked on the noggin by a heavy oar—they cry out *"Oitata!"* and swim off, crying like babies.

The adult Umibōzu will demand a barrel that it can fill with water to flood the ship.

Make sure the barrel has no bottom, and the Umibōzu will spend hours vainly trying to fill the barrel before growing bored and swimming away!

That said, when sailors hear Umibōzu's bloodcurdling battle cry of *"Kuya, Kuya"* upon the gentle breeze, they quickly start saying their prayers!

Case Study 997/85u

Japan is said to flout the strict laws set down by the *International Whaling Commission* on the number of whales that may be hunted each year. The Japanese government laughingly claims that whales are caught for "scientific research." (Yeah, right!)

However, sometimes the sea protects its own. Here is a report from the *Japan Coast Guard* regarding the mysterious sinking of a whaling ship.

Japanese Coast Guard
Marine Accident Brief

Sinking of commercial whaling vessel *Hanta-Kira*

Pacific Ocean, 90 miles west of Aomori, Japan

Investigation Number: 255-MO-4936-009

Investigation Status: Pending

Accident Summary

On February 22 of this year, at approximately 16:10, the Japanese whaling vessel *Hanta-Kira* sank in the Pacific Ocean.

The vessel was three days into a long voyage to the Southern Ocean to commence its annual whaling operations. Of the forty-seven crew members on board, two were rescued, the bodies of eight were recovered, and thirty-seven remain missing and are presumed dead.

Accident Narrative

On February 19, the *Hanta-Kira* departed Aomori Harbor, on the far northern tip of Japan. The ship was armed with one-ton explosive-propelled harpoons, water cannons, acoustic weapons, and stun grenades. The vessel was followed by the antiwhaling vessel *Free Spirit*.

From verbal accounts gathered from members of both vessels, during the third day of the voyage, sometime after 15:40, the captain of the *Hanta-Kira* grew frustrated with the "tiresome animal-lovers" and ordered his men to sink the *Free Spirit*. Stun grenades were fired at the antiwhaling vessel and water cannons were used to try to knock crew members overboard.

According to those interviewed on the *Free Spirit*, the sea had been calm throughout the voyage. Now it began to boil angrily around the *Hanta-Kira*, threatening to flip the vessel over. Dozens of terrified crew members were tossed violently from the deck to disappear beneath the churning waters.

The captain of the *Free Spirit* claims that the sea "rose up like a giant tidal wave, as tall as Mount Fuji," towering above the *Hanta-Kira*. Both captain and crew members insist that it was not an actual tidal wave but "a monstrous black and oily form, with fiery eyes, sharp fangs, flailing tentacles, and the shaven head of a Buddhist monk."

Letting out a "loud roar," this supposed creature leaped upon the *Hanta-Kira*. The vessel was instantaneously "smashed to pieces" by the unprovoked attack, "bursting asunder." The wreckage was pulled under the water as this creature sank once more beneath the sea.

Emergency Response

The Japan Coast Guard (JCG) first received a 406-MHz alert from the *Free Spirit* at 16:31 on February 22. Emergency air rescue vessels were launched to the area. Survivors of the *Hanta-Kira* were picked up and the *Free Spirit* ordered back to harbor. Investigations are continuing.

UMIBŌZU FACT FILE

Location: Japan
Appearance: Giant globular mass with monk's shaven head, among others
Strength: Those the size of a mountain . . . well . . . little Umees, not so much
Weaknesses: Stupidity
Powers: Mighty dumbness
Fear Factor: You're on a small boat far out at sea with nowhere to run . . . pants-filling terrifying, we'd imagine! 71

HOW TO CATCH UMIBŌZU

1. Record the sound of Daisy the cow mooing.
2. Go hunting Umibōzu.
3. When it appears, play back the recording. *Moooooo!*
4. Being kinda dumb, Umibōzu will think your boat is a female Umibōzu and follow you back into the shallows.
5. Unable to swim away, you can catch it easily. (Unless it's the size of a mountain——in which case you're on your own!)

WE... EXAMINER

EW! STRANGE UNEXPECTED BIZARRE and all TRUE

THE WORLD'S MOST RELIABLE NEWSPAPER

GIANT TOAD MENACES BEIJING

EXCLUSIVE REPORT BY NEELA NIGHTSHADE

世界

DEMON BABY LEADS COPS ON 3 STATE CHAS...

PICTURES INSIDE

Lurking beneath the deep lakes and gorges of the Hubei province in the central part of China (capital city Wuhan, hence the name), the *GINORMOUS* Wuhan Toads wait patiently for their prey to appear.

It's not flies and grubs they're hungering for, but lip-smackin' *human flesh*!

Ordinary wild toads will eat at least a thousand insects *per day*. (Yowsers!) One adult human will keep the Wuhnan Toad going all week!

Hubei (湖北 in Chinese or *Húběi* in pinyin—the official system to transcribe Chinese characters and better known as "simplified Chinese" for obvious reasons!) means "north of the lake."

This mountainous forest region is covered in thousands of large and small lakes, especially around the Jianghan Plain. The largest are Hong Lake (134 square miles) and Lake Liangzi (100 square miles).

While their tiny brethren lay up to twenty thousand eggs at a time (double yowsers!), thankfully these titans of the amphibian world only manage to produce a batch of five or six eggs annually—otherwise the entire world would be overrun by giant Wuhan Toads!

With eyes "as big as rice bowls" and a mouth six feet across, these guys are hard to miss (unless you're extremely myopic, and those type of monster hunters don't tend to survive long).

These deadly denizens of the deep have been around since toads and frogs debuted, way back in the Jurassic Period of 199.6 to 145.5 million years ago.

(Nature note: Frogs and toads belong to the scientific order Anura, although frogs are members of the family *Ranidae*, of which there are forty-eight hundred different species. Toads are members of the family *Bufonidae*, which totals five hundred species.)

The Wuhan Toads first came to the attention of the Chinese authorities in 1962. Their existence was immediately concealed from the public on orders of ruthless and brutal dictator Chairman Mao Zedong, aka Mao Tse-tung, aka Chairman Mao (1893–1976), who founded the People's Republic of China in 1949.

A group of drunken fishermen had had a run-in with the Toads days earlier. Deciding to "bomb the heck out of those critters" (our own interpretation of what was said, since we don't speak Chinese and weren't around back then!), they threw numerous sticks of dynamite into one of the lakes.

Understandably, this kind of enraged the Toads, one of which leaped out of the water, screeching angrily. It chased after the men before they jumped into their vehicles and hightailed it out of there.

Upon reporting the incident to the authorities (and before they were locked up in padded cells) the fishermen affectionately nicknamed the creature "Chan." *Ahhh!*

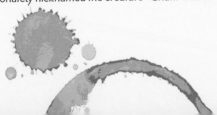

Case Study 117/04wt

Neela Nightshade, ace reporter for the Weekly
World Examiner, recently filed this shocking
report.

Giant Toad Menaces Beijing

Weekly World Examiner Exclusive

BEIJING, China, September 7

Relentless encroachment upon their natural habitat is causing many large
animals to come into conflict with unthinking humans.

Bears, tigers, elephants, and wolves are but a few of the world's most
beautiful creatures that face imminent extinction due to our inherent greed,
our need for living space, and our totally out-of-whack population explosion.

Forget man's inhumanity to man. It's man's inhumanity to the natural world
that will do us in.

Case in point: I have been sent by this paper to investigate sightings of the
extremely shy Wuhan Toad, the so-called "monster" of Hubei province.

The last time a Wuhan Toad had been sighted was back in 1987, when a team of
Chinese scientists hunting this elusive cryptid were attacked.

Mere moments after they set up their cameras, a Wuhan Toad leaped out of a
lake. Its elongated tongue shot out, grabbed a tripod, and the Toad swallowed
it whole!

There have been no more sightings of a Wuhnan Toad—until today!

Hours after arriving in the stifling heat of Beijing, made worse by the
hazardous pollution levels that regularly pass all known danger levels (the
Chinese authorities casually dismiss this as "inclement weather"), I hear

intense screams of utter terror emanating from Tiananmen Square!

Grabbing my camera, I hurry out of my hotel only to be struck down by a tsunami of panicked citizens rushing to escape!

All but trampled to death by the crowd, my only recourse is to roll myself into a ball and wait for the battering barrage of feet to recede.

The brutal assault finally abating, I stagger to my feet, bloodied and bruised. Through blurred vision, I make out an enormous shape three stories high and two stories wide. It lets forth a furious RIBBIT! RIBBIT!

The ensuing decibels are so loud that every window in the surrounding block explodes inward!

Ducking under an awning to save myself from being sliced in two by falling glass, I watch as the Wuhan Toad—for this is what it is—lowers its head and shuffles quickly along the ground, head-butting buildings, bringing them crashing down! Victims aplenty are trampled underfoot!

With Tiananmen Square decimated, and a satisfied RIBBIT!, the Wuhan Toad turns and hops away. It is last reported disappearing into the 404-mile-long Yongding River, its opinion of mankind trespassing upon its isolated habitat powerfully made.

WUHAN TOADS FACT FILE

Location: Hubei province, People's Republic of China
Appearance: Great big huge toad!
Strength: Great big huge toad!
Weaknesses: Gluttony
Powers: Mighty-sticky ten-foot-long tongue; deadly poisonous skin toxins (in case you were thinking of licking one to death)
Fear Factor: 41.4

HOW TO CAPTURE A WUHAN TOAD

ABAIA

Location: Freshwater lakes on the islands of Melanesia. (Melanesia is a subregion of Oceania, and includes most of the islands north and northeast of Australia, including the Solomon Islands, Vanuatu Island, Fiji, and Papua New Guinea.)

Appearance: Ferocious *giant* eel-like beast that protects all creatures in the lakes. If anyone tries to catch a fish, Abaia will thrash its mighty tail, creating a deadly wave to wash away the helpless fisherman. May also call down the rains and create a great flood to sink fishing boats and drown all those aboard.

Strength: It's a freaking giant eel! How powerful do you think it's going to be?!

Weaknesses: Massive depth-charges might do the trick—if it doesn't drown you first!

Powers: Magic, weather control

Fear Factor: 0 or 92. Vegetarians and vegans are, like, totally safe, man. Flesh-eaters on the other hand—you're doomed! (Perhaps time to reconsider your lifestyle choices, eh?)

ACHI KANDIA

Location: Sebou River, Morocco, close to the Aqueduct of Marrakech

Appearance: Malevolent water *djinn* (genie to you and us!) who disguises itself as a beautiful young woman to attract men and bring them close to the edge of the water. Then it changes to its true form—a many-tentacled terrifying giant monster with fangs!

Strength: Seriously scary

Weaknesses: If you manage to run away and meet another human or reach an inhabited place, it can't harm you. However, if caught, prepare to become part of a fish-monster's lunch.

Powers: Magic, shape-changing

Fear Factor: 66.2

BISHOP FISH

Location: Baltic Sea, North Sea, Mediterranean Sea, Black Sea, Aegean Sea

Appearance: Part man, part fish, the size of a short adult human, with an elongated head similar to a bishop's miter (hat). Has a scaly body, clawed flippers, and a large fin that can wrap around the creature like a clergyman's cloak. First caught in 1433 and presented to the king of Poland. A second was netted in Germany in 1533. A third, off the coast of Turkey in the 1990s. Described and illustrated in Volume 4 of Conrad Gesner's best-selling *Historiae animalium* (*Histories of the Animals*), published during 1551–1558.

Strength: Belief in God

Weaknesses: Fishing nets, pollution, predatory sea creatures

Powers: Prayer

Fear Factor: 1 (Aww, come on! They're so cute! But remember, they have God on their side, so no messing around!)

CHAMP

Location: Lake Champlain, amid New York and Vermont in the US and Quebec in Canada. (Champlain is a 125-mile freshwater lake)

Appearance: Scaly or smooth snake or serpent's body, length ten to 187 feet, long neck, flat or round head, horned or moose-type antlers, elephant ears, no ears, red or tan mane, alligator jaws, one to five arching humps, two fins or no fins, four flippers or no flippers, webbed feet or no feet, glowing or "dinner plate" eyes. Color: brown, dark brown, olive, dark brownish olive, black, gray, black and gray, black and brown, black and brown and gray, moss green, dark head and white body, drab or shiny coloring. (Basically, take your pick!) Usually appears between late spring and early fall. Over three hundred reported sightings of Champ since the 1880s.

Strength: Pretty tough

Weaknesses: Not as popular with tourists as Nessie!

Powers: Like Nessie, as if by magic it never appears clearly in photographs; can shift-shape into a log whenever humans are around!

Fear Factor: 32

DOBHAR-CHÚ

Location: Rivers of Ireland
Appearance: An otter (head) and dog (body) combo with a seven-foot-long neck. It either has silky black fur or slimy smooth black skin. The back end resembles a greyhound. Long thin tail. Large white patch in the middle of its chest. Its large flippers are out of proportion to the rest of the body. Or: It is covered in white or gray fur with a black cross on its back. Both versions have black ear tips. Makes a whistling or haunting screech. Born the seventh cub of an ordinary otter.
Strength: Frightening. Evil and aggressive. Will attack humans and dogs without warning. Grasping their victim tightly, it pulls them into the water. Hunts in pairs. If one is killed, the other will not rest until it has had its revenge!
Weaknesses: None!
Powers: Its fur has magical properties that protect it from any type of injury or attack. Superfast both in water and on land.
Fear Factor: 57.4

GROOTSLANG

Location: Richtersveld region, South Africa. The Grootslang lives in a deep cave that connects to the sea forty miles away. Locals call the diamond-filled cave the Bottomless Pit and/or the Wonder Hole. Grootie can also be found chillin' in freshwater rivers and gooey swamps, especially in the Republic of Benin, West Africa.
Appearance: Gargantuan elephant's head and long serpent's body forty feet long and three feet wide
Strength: Hmm, let's think. Monster elephant + Gigantic serpent = Wow!!
Weaknesses: Food—it needs to eat at least sixteen hours a day. Unlike its gentle herbivore cousin, this terrifying creature is partial to chomping down on other elephants . . . and especially yummy humans! In 1917, über-rich English businessman Peter Grayson went off on an expedition to hunt down the Grootslang to show his pals what a really cool dude he was. He was never seen again!
Powers: Speed-swimming; can blow really neat water bubbles out of its trunk
Fear Factor: 44.9

INKANYAMBA

Location: Migratory, although generally lives in the northern forests of KwaZulu-Natal, South Africa, in the deep pools of the three hundred-foot waterfall known as *Howick Falls*. Also found in the Mkomazi River, the Midmar Dam (and its 4,420-acre reservoir), and farm dams in the Dargle area of the Midlands.

Appearance: Monstrous serpent with antelope's or horse's head (sometimes it has more than one head), prominent fore flippers, finned crest or mane, and large wings.

Strength: In times past, the Zulu and Xhosha tribes would annually throw a young virgin girl off the top of *Howick Falls* to appease Inkayamba and stay its mighty wrath, so odds are it's rather a tough dude!

Weaknesses: Uh . . .

Powers: Once a year leaves its lair to find a mate and/or do battle with a rival. Flying on a large and ferocious storm cloud, it creates violent tornados and releases catastrophic deluges of rain and hail that flood the land, killing numerous people in the process.

Fear Factor: The Zulus refuse to even say its name aloud—that's how scary this beastie is! To the Zulu and Xhosa tribes, 99.9. (Although if you're living in Trenton, New Jersey, you're relatively safe!)

KAPPA

Location: Almost every river in Japan (and that's a lot of rivers!)

Appearance: Size of a small child with grotesque lizard-type features. The Kappa is one of many Japanese *suijin* (water people). They love to leap out of rivers to eat or drown humans, especially young children.

Strength: Not impressive; they can be easily shaken off

Weaknesses: Kinda embarrassing: cucumbers. Yep, that shriveled green fruit that's made up of more than 90 percent water is the Kappa's Achilles heel. It can't get enough of them. Wave one in its face and its eyes glaze over, it begins to drool and it is heard to loudly groan "Kyyyyy-uuuuu-riiiiiiiii!" (Kyuri being the Japanese name for cucumber.)

Powers: Strong swimmer. Extremely knowledgeable about medicine. Most of the medical breakthroughs of the Edo period came from Kappas swapping medicine recipes for cucumbers. (Them boys and their cucumbers!)

Fear Factor: 6 (And that's being overly generous!)

LUSCA

Location: Island of Andros, the Bahamas. These deadly creatures live in the spectacular "blue holes" on the island. (Formed during the ice ages of the last million years or more, they look like huge blue pools of still water.)

Appearance: Terrifying half shark/half octopi or half squid/half eel combo. Some rabid newspaper reports claim it's a "dragon-like" creature. Others, that it's a many-headed monster. It may even be a shape-shifter. because anyone who runs into one doesn't live to tell the tale! Lusca is between seventy-five feet (a minnow) to 200 ft long. Razor-sharp teeth and a mass of ginormous multi-suckered tentacles. Voracious predator of humans.

Strength: What do you think?!

Weaknesses: You could try the "trout-tickling" method. Tickle Lusca on its belly and it may go into a trance-like state so that you can pull it onto dry land. (Please advise next of kin before attempting this method.)

Powers: Propulsion swimmer, mega-mega strong, can change color (okay, not much of a power, but still cool!)

Fear Factor: 93.7

NINYGO

Location: Lives in beautiful palaces beneath the seas of Japan.

Appearance: Female water fairy. Half human (the top half, sometimes beautiful, sometimes bestial and monkey-like— even dog-like!), half carp fish (the bottom end). Long scaly arms ending in claws.

Strength: Weak

Weaknesses: Cannot speak, or will only speak to trick her captor into releasing her. Then has a voice like a skylark or a whistling flute.

Powers: Shape-shifting. Very seductive. A Ningyo can appear as a beautiful, kimono-clad young woman on shore, luring men into the water with her sweet song. She then transforms into a giant jellyfish and kills them!

Ningyo either cry tears of pearls, or else will not cry because if one ever does, she will turn human. Eating a Ningyo can bring one extended life, up to eight hundred years or more. The downside being that capturing a Ningyo brings powerful storms and bestows ultra bad luck to her captor. (So, basically, eight hundred years of the worst grief imaginable. Oooh, can't wait!) If a Ningyo is found washed up on shore, it means that a terrible war or calamity is on its way!

Fear Factor: 52

OGOPOGO

Location: Lake Okanagan, British Columbia, Canada.

Appearance: Long, undulating serpent's body. fifteen to seventy long, two feet wide, with a sheep, goat, or horse head. Large eyes, blunt nose, and whiskers resembling a beard. Two horns; jagged fins along the length of its back. Dark green or black scales. Four six-inch flippers. Long forked tail. Ogopogo was a demon-possessed man who committed a murder. The angry Indian gods transformed him into a hideous lake serpent so that he would always remain at the scene of his misdeed and feel eternal remorse.

Strength: Have you ever seen a humongous sea serpent that wasn't phenomenally powerful?! If so, we want to meet him!

Weaknesses: Like Nessie and Champ, he's another show-off water serpent. Oggie loves having his picture taken! Too bad all the thousands of people who claim to have seen the creature are such useless photographers! All those kazillions of pictures come out decidedly blurred!

Powers: Can swim up to forty miles per hour. Really good at eating humans!

Fear Factor: The real N'ha-a-itk is a terrifying behemoth who will happily chew you up and spit out your bones. 79

VODIANOI

Location: Rivers and wells. Vodianoi can be found in most of the Slavic countries. Vodianoi live in underwater palaces built from sunken ships.

Appearance: These guys are cool, because they combine both water beast and undead in one easy package! They are old men with long green beards, and their bodies are covered in scales, hair, and slime. They are the lost spirits of the unclean dead.

Strength: Strong

Weaknesses: Emptying the river or well dry will mess up their evil plans!

Powers: They will wait patiently for a passing swimmer, then pull the victim under the water to drown them. The Vodianoi then turns the now-deceased zombified person into a slave. Won't harm fishermen and millers, who they prefer to befriend and hang out with. Can transform into a fish.

Fear Factor: 63.3